Charles Carrick

Poems

Serious, Humorous and Satirical

Charles Carrick

Poems
Serious, Humorous and Satirical

ISBN/EAN: 9783337397692

Printed in Europe, USA, Canada, Australia, Japan

Cover: Foto ©Andreas Hilbeck / pixelio.de

More available books at **www.hansebooks.com**

DEDICATED

BY

PERMISSION

TO

THE RIGHT HONOURABLE

LORD ATHLUMNEY.

CONTENTS.

viii CONTENTS.

CARRICK'S POEMS.

GOD BLESS THE QUEEN.

God bless the Queen, and save our land
   From foes or foreign power ;
E'en by Thine own Almighty hand
   O crown her happy hour.
Yea, let Thy smile of glowing love,
   And sweet renewing grace,
Uplift her soul in light above,
   Such holiness to trace—
   To reflect her Maker's face.

God bless our land to holiness ;
   Raise England high in power ;
Shower down Thy blessings—crowning bliss
To give true peace and happiness
   From throne to cottage bow'r.

God bless the Queen ! long may she live
   In wisdom-light to shine,
To rule her people and to give
   All praise to Thee divine.

B

O crown her with Thy holy love,
     A living star of light,
That she may reign with Thee above.
     In holiness delight.

ON THE DEATH OF HIS ROYAL HIGHNESS THE PRINCE CONSORT.

O IMMORTAL Prince !
Thou'rt gone to sleep—and sweet be thy repose !
Heaven grant thee bright ethereal joy,
The crown of life—eternal rest in God !
Thy consolation, O most noble Queen !
Is in thy country's love and sympathies ;
For one life-song of universal praise
Is offered up to God in thy fair name.
     Father of Heaven, who can understand
Thy glorious dispensation—life in death ?
How hard it seems to part from those we love !
Yet such is law—Thy will of holy power.
E'en monarchs must obey the call of death.
Yet all things speak delight and heav'nly joy ;
E'en in death is constancy divine.
When Heaven decrees, O much-loved Queen,
Thou'lt meet thy partner in the realms above
In glorious joy of immortality.

CHARLES DICKENS.

Though thou'rt gone,
Thy venerated name shall live
Through ages—ah, to find
The yet unborn love-praise will give
For works thou'st left behind.
Thy usefulness, pre-eminent,
Hath cheer'd the wise—ay, more :
For love and labour thou wert sent,
To teach both rich and poor.
Yea, glorious and immortal Friend.
Thy works reflect thy light,
And give new charms that never end
In memory's sweet delight.

August 26th, 1870.

THE GAME AT WAR.

With two great "gamesters" there can be no sin
To kill ten thousand little men ; but then
The widows and the orphans—what can they,
With those surviving brothers on half-pay,
Possess?—to climb the dust-heap ; ah ! to sway
Their warlike trophies, and to pass away
Into the presence of that One who made
Man not for slaughter. 'Tis His holy will
That kings should not set up the butcher's trade.
Hath He not said, alas ! "Thou shalt not kill?"

August 4th, 1870.

B 2

THE WIDOW AND ORPHANS.

FRAGMENT.

Alas ! alas !
"O where is he ?" the orphan children cry,
    " Our father dear ;" so anxiously to learn.
The mother weeps, but cannot tell them why
    They must not hope, alas ! for his return.
With swelling heart, the tear-drop on the cheek.
    The mother looks into each darling's face
To read her sorrow ; then she turns to weep.
    In prayerful thought of Him who giveth grace,
Sustaining power (to soothe the troubled heart)
    To do her best to understand her trust
And reconcile this truth--that all must part,
    Each one in turn ; for what is man but dust?
Though bright the image fixed upon her mind,
    And sweet the memory of the one all love,
So dear to those poor orphans left behind,
    Who seem to see their father crowned above.

THE MAYOR OF CANTERBURY, HENRY HART, ESQ.

God bless our worthy mayor !
For many honoured friends are moved
In glowing admiration for
His catholic, unsectarian spirit
Which animates both rich and poor
To cradle one so much beloved.

August 20*th*, 1870.

1870.

Turn o'er a new leaf; O the happy new year
May lift up the downcast to dry up the tear;
The rich and the poor, both seeking one end,
To do good for each other, each neighbour and friend.

Turn o'er a new leaf; let us all happy be,
Content with our lot in the blest seventy;
From envy and malice free, from grudging each other,
Let each smile in the help of each kind-hearted brother.

Turn o'er a new leaf; yes, ye far-better-faring,
What worth is the fruit that is e'er given sparing?
The abundance and worth must prove what is good—
The fruit is not known by its beautiful wood.

Turn o'er a new leaf, ere the tree becomes bare;
Neglect of that one thing may bring on despair:
Let age rather come, e'en to dignified worth,
Than failing in beauty and be smiling in mirth.

REFLECTIONS IN THANINGTON CHURCHYARD.

Behold the tombs, the new-made graves between,
The house of prayer, the hallowed ground; I ween
But few can pass this holy tranquil scene
Unconscious of its summer-smiling flowers,
Rejoicing in the light of Godly powers;
The star-like daisies in perfection seem
To smile a welcome, each a starlight queen.
Why come they forth to live but for an hour

To honour and to grace? Mark where ye tread !
Crush not the living, smiling o'er the dead
With life-all-cheering, emulating power,
And whilst time flies to bring the closing hour
To flowers of beauty, and to show His will
By certain laws which nature must fulfil !

     But Summer's gone ; her brightest day is past !
Oh, shall *we* find a brighter day at last,
Travelling each one to his grave so fast ?

     Oh, where are they—the flowers now unseen ?
Hushed to sleep by Autumn's downcast sigh
But to escape the winter morning keen
When shrubs or trees of larger growth may die,
To mark the foot-prints where death shall have trod,
And bid us watch the working hand of God.

     Flowers ! where are they ? echo now replies
" Watch, wait until the churchyard stars arise :
In living beauty they will smile again
To bud and bloom and glorify His name !"

     Why look we forward to the coming spring,
When kindly nature shall awake to sing
Her universal anthem to our King,
And spread her gifts, and many blessings bring ?
'Tis then the earthly stars will smile delight,
And heavenly ones shall give forth brighter light,
To cheer the heart of man and glad his eye,
And still to teach him how to live and die !

     Where are the flowers that lived but for a day,
Smiling in death e'en as they passed away,
From change to life, to beauty from decay ?

Here in the churchyard then, O man, take heed,
And strive to learn His lesson, for indeed
'Tis here a man of care can find his way
To learn that lesson on the churchyard sod.
Humbled though guided by His loving rod,
He must reflect, repent, and look to God!

December 14th, 1869.

THE POWER AND LIGHT OF TRUTH.

THE man
Of honest heart, who seeketh but the Truth,
    That's fitful as the very life that's given ;
In holiness it glorifies his youth ;
    In age uplifts him to the joys of Heaven.

August 6th, 1870.

REFINED ENVY AND JEALOUSY.

FRAGMENT.

WITH seeming
Unsuspicious mind, the jealous fool
    Will cringe and fawn, so warmly to beset
With every kindness, yet complain how cool
    The gentle one (entangled in his net).

The double-face of envy (ah, how true !)
    Resemble both the angels, good and evil ;
The secret stab, and then a smile for you.
    Must crown the goodness of the one so civil.

Alas! such goodness; he who can discern
   The double-face should always first with grace
'To meet the foe with gentleness to learn,
   That envy is but of the human race.

HEAVEN OUR HOME.

"In my Father's house are many mansions; if it were not so,
I would have told you. I go to prepare a place for you."—
JOHN xiv. 2.

THERE is a home, a heavenly home,
   Where death can never come,
Beyond the grave—the clouds afar,
   Where immortal spirits roam.

There is, indeed, a blessed home,
   And heavenly garden scene,
Where joy, and peace, and love abound
   In harmony serene.

Onward, through the path of life,
   Midst the storms arise—
Seek that garden scene of flowers
   Which blooms beyond the skies.

Who would not wish, ay, strive to gain,
   That garland love divine,
Of living, holy, heavenly flowers,
   Which earth could never twine?

Fast fly the moments, linger not ;
   We'll hasten to that happy home ;
We'll clothe ourselves in robes of light,
   And heaven will bid us come.

That happy home—that better world—
   Where peace for ever reigns ;
Ah ! there our loving friends in God
   Have written down their names.

Look up, behold them in their joy,
   In prayer look up to Him ;
We'll praise Him in our morning song
   And heavenly evening hymn.

The holy good on sacred ground,
   Through the darksome night,
Are guided by the stars above
   To their blest home of light.

Our friends, e'en dearest friends, are there,
   For whom our tears were shed ;
Too dear, too good to live on earth,
   They died, but are not dead.

They live in sunshine—new delight—
   No sorrow, care, nor sigh,
Beyond the grave, a life of joy,
   No tears to swell the eye.

They live in vivid lustre, shine
   As stars of Heaven, as bright,
To guide us in our onward course
   Through dark and dreary night.

Round about the gate of Heaven,
  They shine in spiritual love,
They're only dim when we forget
  They shine for us above.

Who would not seek those endless joys,
  Improve the time that's given,
And weep with those who weep on earth—
  Rejoice with them in Heaven ?

Arise to glory, home of glory,
  Death is life's awakening duty,
Changed to be unchanged for ever;
  Changed to heavenly beauty.

The day will soon be spent, alas !
  To-morrow, all the earthly blossom,
As withered grass, must fade and die,
  The soul still living unforgotten.

Hark ! the mournful church bell tolling ;
  Some loved brother just gone home ;
All is silent in death's glory,
  Whilst God bids each one to come.

BEREAVEMENT.

Oh, can the distress'd,
Bereft, fond mother see her child above
  Smiling in the arms of Him whose eye
Is fixed upon her! ah, in pitying love,
  To change her heart (and make her fit to die)
  And give her faith to see her boy on high,
  In smiling light of all eternity!
He lives—she knows he lives; her heart is full,
Watching and waiting now her cup is full:
For now she looks beyond the grave: her choice
  Is death, to rise and meet her child above :—
In prayerful joy she seems to hear his voice
  Whilst in the arms of Him who is all love.

KIND WORDS.

Kind words of gentle breathing love
  Uplift the sadden'd heart to give
New pleasures—ah, that smile above,
  To teach us all how we should live.
    As the voice of angel-breathing,
      Oh, such noble virtues trace ;
    As in joy and memory pleasing
      Bring to view the Saviour's face.

Words of sympathetic love
  Crown the joy of future light ;
Such the living God above
  Recognises with delight.

Words of loving-kindness given
    Mark the rich and poor as one ;
Such on Earth is life in Heaven ;
    In other words, His " Kingdom come."

DIGNIFIED HYPOCRISY.

THE hypocrite who prays aloud is one
    To show effective skill, to cause alarm,
To make impressions—ay, but then why shun
    These polished reptiles that can do no harm ?

Like mountebanks at some small country fair,
    They bow and scrape to mimic all around,
Assuming all that's good in pompous air,
    But then of course their object's easy found.

We hear them chatter with an ugly smile,
    And cut a dash, and show they have a cheek.
To prove their "shakey" state till some loose tile
    May fall upon our corns to make us speak.

Religious pride is only meant for swells
    Who show unerring skill in pomp and pride,
Who neither hear the preacher nor the bells,
    And only go to church but to deride.

Poor ignorant creatures ! oh, before we part,
    Let them be warned (by one who's no ill will)
To trifle not with Him who knows the heart,
    And can, alas ! the soul and body kill.

August, 1870.

WAR! WAR!

A FRAGMENT.

> " Farewell,
> Thou pure impiety, thou impious purity ;
> For thee I'll lock up all the gates of love."

WE fight against the proud :
The crafty, envious, never can find rest,
The arbitrary never shall be blest,
No matter tho' in scarlet robes he's dress'd,
Rings on each finger, stars upon his breast—
Revengeful, cruel, yea, alas ! a cheat,
A fool of pride, perfection, and deceit,
Full of lifeless pleasure, he honours craves,
　Selfish in th' extreme, obtrusive brave,
　　But when he dies no friend to cry " Oh, save !"
No one to weep for his departed worth ;
　No one to look with pity on his grave ;
　　Yet gladly find a place for such a knave.
Such ignorant men arise above their station,
　To show their understanding by their skill ;
Perplexed with men of light and education,
　Who'd honour them had they but got the will.
Sometimes, by way of joke, they show respect
　To such illnatured dolts whom none can please,
Whose powerful claret-wine we all reject,
　　Yet praise them for the richness of their cheese :
　　But such a one may wish to live at ease.
　　His pure delight is meanness whilst he lives :
　　To get all, keep all, whilst he nothing gives.

But dread and sorrow to his friends around,
Where murder or vile slavery abound.
Such gloom, alas! in action no good brings:
In wounding others his own conscience stings
His very soul until he's laid to sleep—
Down among the dead men, down so deep;
Whilst others live, alas! reflect and weep.
In this enlightened day there may be found
The hateful tyrant on forbidden ground:
We scorn his glory as we take a glance,
Prepare to meet the foe should he advance.
Like David, we defy the giant race:
In strength and courage meet him face to face;
In holy war we fight for him above;
And should we kill, 'tis simply out of love.

＊——

THE PASSING HOUR.

Christmas, 1869.

THE "golden rays" of sun are past,
The dreaded change has come at last,
The rain and snowflakes falling fast—
Where are the flowers (oh! winter's blast)
            To smile on Christmas Day?

That day has pass'd, the "snow" is gone,
And January's pressing on,
To usher in a brighter morn
Of sunbeam-smiling joys new-born,
            Alas! to pass away.

Yes, Time is on the wing. to spread
Great gifts that man may raise his head,
In hope, ah yes ! to banish dread,
E'en whilst he contemplates the dead,
    He learns of Him to pray.

What little time he has for thought,
Here each one knows his day is short,
To mark the lesson Nature's taught—
To prove all things must come to nought,
    And man to crumbling clay.

Can his immortal soul then rise,
In gratitude beyond the skies,
To Him who is all truth, all-wise,
Midst hope and fear, or tears and sighs,
    And humbled to obey.

That Holy One who giveth light
To watch the changes of the night,
In prayer to set himself aright,
Man finds his end is but delight
    To await the Judgment Day.

"THE TRUE VINE."

BEHOLD the living Vine !
See her branches how they flourish,
Giving fruit that cannot perish
  In His light divine.

SMILING CHARITY.

BLEST charity,
Wherever poverty is found
    The Angel-love is there,
To wipe the tear, console, and cheer
    With tenderness and care ;
And but to give from her small store,
    Her help in gentle love,
To find (returning gratitude)
    Life's blessings from above.

"LIFT UP YOUR HEADS."

SERVE God and live,
Ye honest rich, industrious poor,
    Seek not the world's applause,
But let your light shine more and more
    To glorify His laws.
Heed not the praises of great men,
    Who flatter thee to bring
Real pleasure of the world ; for then
    'Twill leave a deadly sting.
But lift your heads, both rich and poor,
    In prayer to Him above ;
So let your light shine evermore
    In holiness and love.

" HAPPY PAIR."

OH blissful morn !
Hail, "wedded pair !"—the Arabs' music-horn
Has drawn together all the "wise" that vied
With pitying friends who come to raise a storm,
To "kill" the bridegroom,* just to save the bride.

CONVERSATION.

THIS cheering task will gain approving smile—
Talk well and to the purpose to enforce
The earnest truth, the life of thy discourse,
In noble words to mimic none in style.

LAMENT.

" IN that still voice "—
Hark th' awaken'd sinner's sigh,
Whilst preparing here to die :
How loving tears are shed,
In anxious thought and natural dread
Upon a sleepless sorrowing bed,
Is known to Him on high.
But He hears the sinner's cry ;

* His effigy drowned in the River Stour.

C

'Tis the Saviour stops the way.
" Look to Me," we hear Him say ;
" All thy troubles cast away ;
    In faith and hope, oh learn to pray,
    In holiness thy time employ ;
    Sorrow shall be turned to joy :
        Canst thou see the land of light,
        Of eternal sweet delight ?
        Enter there and find thy rest
        With the living and the blest."

"OUR DEATH-DOOMED FRIENDS."

DEATH'S arrows fly, with warning power,
But fear them not ! wisely, yea, most wisely,
Death's sent by God to give new birth and life
Of immortality.   " His will be done."
    Fear not, weep not, O ye afflicted friends,
Tho' the " loving ones " be snatched from thee :
It is the call of Him who gives man life—
Preserves his soul to all eternity.
Why wish to spend more time with trifles here ?
Why fear because, alas ! the time is short ?
Eternity of joy and love of Heaven
Cannot be gained unless we die in God.
Come, yea come, ah ! quickly come, O death,
If it is the holy will of God.

For He will give us grace, in mercy smiles,
To follow those dear loved ones gone before.
Yea, as His pitying care is full of love,
Let us prepare to meet the King of kings.
Hail! heavenly love of transitory joy;
O banish from the soul every sorrow,
And take us up on high.
                Hark! the death-knell!
Ha! another and another friend is gone.
Oh God of love and mercy, life and death,
Thou knowest what is best. Weep not, alas!
The swollen eye, the tear-drop on the cheek
Speak that inward sorrow of the heart
For loss of worldly gain and worldly love,
Which shows but dimly in the light of faith
And hope in God. Rather rejoice to die—
To live again in heavenly joy eternally.

THE IGNORANT PROUD.

THE ignorant,
"Stuck up," very poor and proud,
  Must think he's wondrous clever,
To ape the monarch of his race—
  Disguise his idol ever.

For worldly fame he struts about,
  To show his peacock-breeding;
Delights to hear the "greenhorn" shout,—
  Pride, ignorance succeeding.

His every virtue to display,
  In *light* of ostentation,
The "long ears" with the natural "bray"
  Must gain some approbation.

Whilst from the dust-hole to the grave
  He labours on for "glory,"
To find his "trappings" with his "light"
  Is only transitory.

THE IMPENITENT THIEF.

ALL that's bad,
Involved in so much crime,
  The harden'd thief in deep distress
Hath made bad use of time.
  He now must suffer : no redress;
    The jovial rogue can shed no tear ;
    In his distress no one is near,
    Neither can he hope nor fear—
No thought : he seeks for death to save
Him from the prison.   But the grave
Almost refuses such a knave,
    Whose name no one will hear.
      Impenitent, how could he see—
        To find a Saviour to atone ?
        A wanderer without a home,
        Lost for ever, left alone,
        To repent, to weep and moan.
      Through all eternity.

August 1st, 1870.

GLORIOUS SONGSTERS.

ILLUSTRIOUS crow of joy-delusive hope,
Sing on, thou mournful bard, quickly arise !
    Life's melancholy state would'st thou prolong,
Thy jarring strains distract beneath the skies,
    United with the doleful cricket's song,
Whose banishment, ah, ah, alas ! what grief !
    The grasshopper may gladden by his lay ;
Sing on, then, cheerful insect (give relief)
    Beyond the stars, or whither would'st thou stray ?
To prison-gloom, beneath the wild-topped heath—
    How many singing insects there unknown,
To sicken each one by his song in death.
    Ay, hark the spiders' death-watch, how they moan !
Listen to their dying fate, what gloom !
    Whilst over singing birds the cricket reigns ;
Would man, then, listen whilst he builds his tomb.
    Preferring death to such discordant strains ?
Oh, grasshopper, ill-fated bard of light,
    To rise above—in sorrow to be drown'd ;
Ah, no ; thy living cutting notes delight
    (In mutual anguish, solitude profound)
Birds and insects that have no command
    O'er their jarring sweet spontaneous lays :
Under the rose they find throughout the land
    Protection 'neath the thorny, briery maze.

DOWN AMONG THE DEAD.

FRAGMENT.

OLD times have passed away to find
Ten thousand gods of ev'ry kind,
The spotless garment thrown aside,
The wise and learned side by side—
Disunited quacks preside.
Dissenting talk in "glowing-fire"
    Combine to raise a Babel-Tower,
    Disregarding wisdom-power,
Confounding as they rise still higher.
    Is there one true spirit-church?
        And is not Christ the head?
    Though not of wise men in research
        Down among the dead.

How many converts are at ease
Since man possess'd the heav'nly keys !
Blind leading blind, alas ! to fall,
" Jangling " they hear not His call ;
On self alone they all depend,
Each one below, a guide and friend :
He spends his "glory" and his time
In turning virtue into crime.

EDUCATION—RELIGIOUS KNOWLEDGE.

It is a joyous power of light
   That crowns immortal youth,
And elevates with pure delight
   The tender growth of truth.

Religious knowledge seeks to prove
   The power of new creation,
That change of heart (outpouring love)
   Is gained by education.

The first lisp'd prayer of any child
   May prove that wisdom's given,
With smiling grace, ah, to prepare
   The little one for Heaven.

ENLIGHTENED STUPIDITY.

See that great man
Climb the highest point, where none hath trod ;
   But then his " larnin' " raises him so high ;
Whilst empty praises of the world—how odd !—
To make the " booby " *think* he is a god :
   He builds of course his " mansion " in the sky,
There to live in wretchedness of gloom,
   To find his " airy castle's " but a *tomb.*

HEAVENLY RICHES.

FROM the very poor
The gifts that most delight
Are (like the widow's mite)
   Where honest poverty is known :
The poor live for each other ;
   There the kindly hand extends
To help a needy brother.
   In gentle sympathetic love
The smallest trifle given
   Only shows by light above
Their riches are in Heaven.

THE BRAGGART.

THE " boaster,"
Without incessant talk how could he live
   To tell his " million friends " (all he *would* say)
About *his* " wealth ;" *his* " worlds of gold ?" he'd give
   E'en Heaven itself, so full of ri ch display,
   To rob a friend, to help a scheming foe,
   Only in light of ostentatious show.

FALSE GUIDES.

IF "lying is a virtue,"
Then let the "wise quacks" falsely teach,
'Twill only leave them in the lurch ;
The few who go to hear them preach
Do not belong to any church.
But knaves and fools can do no harm,
Nor can the "stuck-up" *wise*,
Because there is a stronger arm
That will not let them rise
To propagate their lies.

VANITY OF CONCEIT.

THE well-dress'd fops of ostentatious show
Must strut about, and who would dare condemn
Our "swellish gents," whose *brilliant light* we know
Must show that they are not "*conceited* men ?"

"BEHOLD THE LAMB OF GOD.'

BEHOLD the Lamb,
Whose blood, alas ! was shed,
Yet He has risen from the dead.
Follow Him, the " Lamp of light,"
In holiness of pure delight ;
Behold the glory of His face.

Sinner, look on Him whilst near ;
Why longer doubt in trembling fear ?
It is the blessed Saviour dear.
Follow Him now in the race :
First secure His saving grace,
Then worship Him the one adored—
'Tis no other than the Lord.
　　His hands and wounded side—oh trace
　　The scars that dim His holy face.
Lift up thy weeping eyes—
Reality throws off disguise—
　　Doubt not 'tis He who gives delight,
　　The star of everlasting light.
O follow Him, the Lamb of love,
To life and holiness above—
　　　　To all eternity.

FRAGMENT.

Father, Friend, thou Giver of all good,
Blest Comforter of never-ending bliss,
In light of mercy Thou upholdest man
To be exalted and to harmonize
In holiness—the Spirit Truth of life.
　　What endless blessings smiling from above !
(For man, alas ! whilst living for the world)
The saving grace of His redeeming love
Designs to change the heart and fit for Heaven.

" BLACK SHEEP."

THESE " righteous rogues " must live in faith to shine,
  In hope to gain a sure reward some day,
If only they can spend their ill-used time
  To cure the " wretches " that can never pray.
Such saintly preachers of angelic mind
  Would only " swindle " to become as great,
High in rank and dignity refined,
  As those who never had a name or state.
Pretending genius, gift divine, the giant nigger
Rises in pride to show his noble figure,
  And prove his oratorial powers sublime
To lead astray the poor " black sheep," and prove
That " righteous rogues " must have a kind of love,
  And that their love must really be divine.

VANITY AND VICE.

THOSE who assume great virtue without light,
  And hold their heads above the wicked crowd,
Too stiff to stoop to exercise their right,
  With those who are too honest to be proud—
Are *wise* indeed for being " over-nice,"
In sanctifying vanity and vice.

BAD CONDUCT IN CHURCH.

A REBUKE.

YE singing men, or brother worms, mark him
Who whilst at church dare carry out his plan
To " beat for time," and whisper when he can :
Blest little lambs of light, would ye be fed
On wisdom's pride to show ye are well-bred ?
Then learn a lesson from the living-dead,
And pay attention whilst the Book is read—
To all that may in holiness be said
To guide us in our conduct by the rule
Of holy faith, progress like little men
Or simpletons.   But why denounce the fool
Who's paid to do his " duty ?"—ay, but then
One's singing should be worthy of his school,
Whose simple part is brawling out " Amen."

SMALL BOYS OF THE PERIOD.

WITH their bibs on,
We meet our " future men," and give them room
To strut about the streets and look so wise—
Cut from their mothers' apron-string too soon :
There's nothing they can do that will surprise-
Although of course one scarce believes his eyes.
Each little " Arab " shows how he can rise

To fill his pipe—his vitals to consume ;
Transformed a " man," to inhale the fume
Of " 'bacca."   But then it is no joke
To see an infant stifled in his smoke.

FLATTERY.

These vile pretenders, who are over-wise,
  Would make us tremble whilst they overrate us ;
They'd cringe and fawn, or flatter to surprise ;
  They're sure to offend whene'er they would delight us.

THE MODERN CRITIC.

The immaculate scribe
Whose logic, wit, and genius, tho' " first rate,"
  Can equal not his wisdom nor his skill ;
His word can raise an idiot high in state,
  Or make the kingdom tremble at his will.
  Ay, mark the startling essays from his quill :
He teaches by his light the blind to see,
  The sickly, lame, to climb Parnassian steep.
Behold the critic ! see what dignity
  And learning there is in a common sweep.
Will not the " Brilliant Future " crown his fame
With something more than just—an empty name ?

PETTY SCANDAL.

HEED not
The niggling, cunning, gifted prater,
Who seldom thinks of his Creator ;
Whose vulgar talk (or stock in trade)
Is to do mischief and persuade
His kindred blockheads now to rise
And gain repute for telling lies ;
To injure those who little know
Why each good friend becomes a foe
By secret scandal down below.

What are the attributes of those
Whose real perfection no one knows—
Who for distinction only rise
To prove their " gentle hints " are wise ?
Each busybody magnifies
His brothers' faults, and with such grace,
To prove his scandal's no disgrace—
Nay, but a virtue in its place—
So natural to the common race.

But such is life, each cunning " cad,"
Beware of him, and think how sad
For one to talk another mad !
Rather let our silence show
We've no connection down below
With those poor piteous demon-haters,
Who claim to be their own creators.

August 23*rd*, 1870.

"JACK IN OFFICE."

" First Jack, then Mr. John, then John, Esquire,"
So by degrees the " noodle " rises higher
Among the class of quacks who live to brag
    Of what they do in office : " When *I* speaks."
'Tis fun to see them puff their dirty shag,
    Yet often have to eat their scented leeks.
The poor man's friend, indeed ! Can we not trace
    These little narrow-minded men of fire,
Who shine in virtue of decaying grace ?
    They'd down with Church to raise the poor man higher.
What could we do without such " larned " men,
    Who're ever seeking for the highest place ?
These cunning blades are always honoured when
    They rise in power to glory in disgrace.

A BRIGHT EXAMPLE.

The " righteous " bigot
Is wise indeed on barren land,
With upturned eyes and outspread hand ;
With such advantage at command,
He builds upon the false quicksand,
      To find a " prize " hereafter.

In ridicule, ah ! man's mistake,
The fool's reward, how few would take,

From him who "puffs" to keep awake,
Or pants for glory (for our sake).
The " movement " makes the temple shake
Until of course our poor sides ache
          With unrelenting laughter.

August 25th, 1870.

———•———

CONTESTABLE POWER OR BEAUTY CONFRONTED.

The Rose and Lily in dispute
    Which should be the queen,
A Daisy and a Buttercup
    Sprang up to intervene :
The Lily pale, incessant ire,
The red-lip virgin full of fire,
    Thus in hot dispute,
And by their envious, noisy deeds
Awak'ning, yea, ten thousand weeds
    From sleep to active duty;
'Twas Nature's power to rebuke—
That weeds should glorify and choke
    Those queenly flowers of beauty.

———•———

THE PREACHER.

" Men look at a man out of the pulpit, to see what he is worth
in it."

GIVE me the man who always speaketh plain—
  Consistent in his acts (resists the proud),
Whose charity is wide, not given in vain,
Who renounces bigots when they speak aloud
  Their repetitions to the busy crowd.

GOOD FOR EVIL.

FOR every evil good thou should'st return,—
To weak, vain fools whose intellect's keen,
Whose guilty conscience is not over clean,
Whose life and acts, contemptible and mean,
To show that their true estimate is known,
As barking dogs that snap at every bone—
Running at large and growling when they can
  Cannot insult an honest well-bred man.

August 17*th*, 1870.

FAITH, HOPE, AND CHARITY.

THERE is that *faith* which sets man free,
  Whose " works " are known above,
And crowns the honest heart to see
  His smile-approving love.

D

There is that *hope* for such who raise
    Themselves by truth in grace,
Whilst in the " race " they sing His praise
    To find a resting-place.

There is that *charity* which finds
    Real comfort from above,
And joys that fill enlightened minds
    With holiness of love.

1868.

FRAGMENT.

" Come unto Me all ye that are weary, and I will refresh you."

         FAINT and weary ?
Come to the Holy Feast, the Table's spread
For sinners.

         Yes, for *all* His blood was shed ;
Meditate in holiness ; 'tis right
To eat, drink, in faith of living light,
Feast upon His body.

         What delight,
In smiling blessings of eternal love !
O solemn charms th' rapt'rous soul to move
In pray'r, uplifting soul to life above.

September 16*th*, 1869.

HONEST RESPECTABILITY.

THE man who is inclined to sell his vote
    Must prove himself to be in good possession—
A crown in pocket, perhaps a *borrow'd coat*,
    An honest look, to show his right profession.

"STREET BRAWLERS."

THESE great street brawlers, why are they allowed
    To preach? but hark!
The horrid yelling 'mongst the busy crowd
    Met for a lark,
To whistle, dance, and sing throughout the day,
    And cry for beer,
Whilst very sober men pretend to pray
    As others sneer—
To bring " religion " in contempt, but oh!
    They must be "good;"
Such godly men who only live for show
    Are understood.
Each Pharisee of vain ambitious spark
    May find his joy
To pray aloud or *whisper* in the dark;
    But to decoy
Poor simpletons whene'er they're off their guard,
    There's cruel play—
To be bitten by the serpent may seem hard.
    Then who can pay

These " Pharisees and Scribes ?"—how many join
    To hear them preach
Their startling " truths" in something so divine?
    For who can teach
The way to that dark barren land of night
    Better than they?
Ay, even the ignorant may find delight
    In what they say,
But who shall stop the *righteous* "shouting out"
    Their madd'ning cheers,
To keep in "order" those who never doubt
    Their eyes and ears?
Alas ! these great street brawlers, how they weep
    For all around—
To see not *one* " pure white," but all *black* sheep
    On holy ground !

SINCERITY.

How sweet to dwell on him who doeth right !
    Can such real pleasure ever find its end ?
In holiness creating pure delight
    By sinless love, which proves the honest friend.

OUR GREAT MEN : OR, THE RISING GLORY IN SUBLIME QUACKERY.

THE man of
As many faces and as many names,
   The natural gossip most men live to shun—
   Whilst perfect fools would glorify the fun,
   And praise him for his scandalizing tongue ;
To crown him king, to rule the tattling dames.

Invincible quack, why meddle with the church ?—
   One of his wives should have forbid the banns.
Behold the sweep, now grovelling deep in search
   For diamond coals on barren lands.
   Tho' pure white gloves now hide his dirty hands.
Yet two black objects each in turn we view—
The double changing face is always new.

THE GREATEST FOOL.

IN borrow'd plumes.
The greatest fool in all creation
   Is he who struts to hear his name,
And boast about his education—
   To show the fellow has no brain :
Yet whilst in this he is succeeding,
   Though but to prove his royal state,
The perfect fool must show his breeding,
   Altho' his " wisdom " comes too late.

THE SPIDER AND THE FLY.

SEE the spider,
Never languid, never idle ;
  Mark it in its happy cell :
How delighted with the simple
  "Insect gnat" no one can tell !
See the net-work of the spider,
  And its moral musings there :
How ingenious, how complexed,
  Let the simple "gnat" beware.
    See the danger-web ; ah ! see
    The spider's sensibility,
    The simple fly's stupidity.
See the welcome insect meeting,
  How affection binds the heart !
Little "gnat" the spider greeting !
  In the magic charms of art
  Well the spider plays its part—
  Once entrapped can ne'er depart.
    Foolish gnat—silly fly,
    Insects have a right to die.

1863.

THE MEANEST OF MISERS.

                THIS poor
Dejected wretch, whilst counting out his heap
  Of gold, would sell his " patches," but in hope
  T' enable him to buy a piece of rope
To hang himself, to save his future keep.

USELESS ORNAMENT.

DANE JOHN.

THE cannon's charge could do no more
    Than raise a little dust,
But now it's spik'd and left alone,
    An " ornament" to *rust*,
Why should we wish again to bore
    The *useless* "gun " that's curs'd ?
It's " powers " of course we trust no more,
    For fear the thing would burst.

WHAT IS LIFE ?

FRAGMENT.

GREAT holy God, of infinite power and light !
Look down in pity, raise poor fallen man,
The glorious exalted works of Thy creation.
But what is man that Thou hast made, O God,
In the image of Thyself—of human nature,
Yet possess'd of mind for immortality ?
In faith and prayer he lives to hear of Thee.
Ah, sweet devotion, conscience-giving love,
Of glorious salvation of his never-dying soul.

            Good glorious God !
Pour out Thy Holy Spirit of quick'ning grace.
That new-born power, regenerative light,
To strengthen man in search of heav'nly joy.
Loving, living, smiles of eternity.

But what is life ?   A mere passing shadow.
Yea, life is but a dream ; the day's soon gone,
Silenced in the solemn sleep of night,
To awaken into life immortal power
Of sublime glorious light and beauty,
To be crowned with angel-loving saints of love,
In smiles of God, the all-enlightened Lamb
Of majestic powers.

        Good works in faith,
The Tree of everlasting Truth, shall have
Full growth in Paradise, transplanted there :
Its budding flowers shall never, never die,
But bring forth fruit holy unto God,
E'en in His joyous light of heaven-born glory,
Which cannot pass away.

    Life, what is it, ay, here below on earth?
Man's secret sins are only known to Him
Who is all smiles, all pitying love.   He deigns
His tenderness and mercy ever good
To lift man up beyond this troubled world
Of passing glory.

    Then let us now awake, andlook above,
Watching in preparation for change and death,
In faith and hope, of holiness of joy,
Ere, alas ! we find our earthly grave
Among the dead.

THE WINTER OF THE NEW YEAR.

Pass on, dull Winter,
Let cheering sunlight now new pleasure bring,
  Insects and birds to enliven us with song.
Pass on, pass on, and let the journeying Spring
  Come forth to cheer ; alas, why stay so long !
The trees and shrubs are waiting to expand
  Their bursting buds, to open in full power,
To crown the wisdom of His giving Hand,
  The awak'ning beauty of the budding flower,
The voice of Nature cheereth Time to aid,
  Now in her gladden'd smile we hope and look
For change in glory—Time is not dismayed
  To show the more glorious pictures of her book.
The hand of Time is pointing many ways,
  Whilst Nature's watching full of marked devotion,
And man beholds in ecstacy of praise
  The gifts of God in solemn adoration.

Pass on, dull Winter, yea, now pass away :
  Flowers and fruit e'en Nature now desires ;
It ill-becomes thee to prolong thy stay,
  Whilst the shivering poor are watching without fires,
Trusting in thy quick retirement,
  In Nature's law of rightful government.

January 1866.

ASCENSION DAY.

By the eye of faith in holiness we see
Our Brother Friend the Saviour God ascend
In majesty on high to heavenly, glorious,
Never-ending power.

Glorious solemn truth,
His birth, and life, and rising from the dead
Is crowned by that last glorious act on earth,
His miraculous departure to the realms above
In perpetual glory.

In Heaven He lives,
To plead for simple man, to save the world :
With unabated loving mercy smiles,
He's looking down in pity from above,
Fulfilling His great mission of Redemption,
To save his own poor fallen untaught creatures
From death eternal, never-ending sorrow.

Oh, adoring Providence of eternal power,
Can man overlook God's blessings, and deny
His light in glory power of safe deliverance ?

Arise, arise, to consecrate that day,
In grateful joy, with all the heav'nly host,
The holy redeem'd, the living saints of glory,
Heaven and earth, as one of glorious future.
To sing the praises of the Lamb of God.

TRANSIENT BLISS.

SLEEP on my eyelids gently fell
Whilst musing on the holiness of truth :
I saw a star so gloriously divine,
Full of grace and beauty, full of love,
Smiling sweet affection in the light
Of sublime glory.

   That star of love
Can never be forgotten. Oh, alas !
Amazed and trembling, filled with joy supreme,
Lost in wonder as I gazed above
And beheld His light and glory—
Full of admiration, full of love.
In tenderness of keenly sensibility
I felt a tear dropping from the eye,
Which spoke the silent language of my heart.
My soul thus fill'd—ah, with unearthly joy,
God called me by my name, and I became
As dead ; alas ! awaken'd from my dream
To the world's many sorrows unto death,
To live another day.

THE INFIDEL.

" The fool hath said in his heart, There is no God."

SCORN, nay pity, the " man" who doubts
The *inspiration* of the HOLY SCRIPTURES ;
He refuses THE BOOK, and denies the LIVING GOD.
Tho' everlasting shame be on his brow—yet pity him,

For God, and not *man* is his JUDGE ;
But the candid Christian would ask :
" Why should the evil-disposed infest the earth,
To contaminate the mind of the wavering few,
Who are often too willing to be balanced
In man's detestable scales of injustice,
Simply to avoid the hot displeasure of a fool ?"
But God is merciful to all in this life ;
He causes the sun to shine on the just and unjust.
What a striking proof of His great love Divine !
Divine benevolence, this comprehensive scheme of Christianity,
The heavenly way in which God deals with man.
Shall we not acknowledge these His truths,
That we may all learn to live for a better world ?
Hear our prayers in this, O Lord God of mercy—
Change, O change the heart of the unbeliever.
But it cannot be conceived how a man
Of refined feelings—mind shaped for knowledge,
And sharpen'd by education in this age of inquiry—
Ah, general inquiry and improvement—
Can boldly stand forth and deny his Maker.
Oh ! let him consider the momentary power
And glory of this inferior planet—our blessed earth :
Its wonderful, powerful degree of motion :
This silent, correct, and distant travelling,
This rapidity of more than a thousand miles
In one short minute—ah, year after year.
O that restless active power, order, and time, giving
The varied seasons—Spring, Summer, Autumn, and Winter !
Let him look no further for proof in foolish argument :

This must be sufficient to convince him
Of God's wonderful wisdom and Divine authority.
Ah ! there is indeed an everlasting God ;—
But how detestable to hear a man in boastful language
Striving to overrule and misguide the young,
Denying the truth with seeming candour and judgment,
Often in benevolence of silly outward profession,
Declaiming that the privileges enjoyed here
Are not of God, but chance !   Ah ! what is chance ?
Pity, O pity the man who cannot believe
In this fixed period of light and darkness.
Everything is beautiful and perfect in order.
But, conceited man ! does not the sun and moon shine
To promote the cause of Truth and Light ?
Ah ! the overpowering changes of magnificence
Of DAY and NIGHT—O blessed, blessed God.
But the man who denies the Holy Book of God,
Which was written for his eternal benefit,
Would perhaps strike a medal in honour of his wickedness,
That his illustrious ignorance should be marked.
O man, think of the displeasure of Him
Who can alter and change all things !
But, O may darkness, where light is, never revisit
This land of already beset snares !
O let us " enlist under the banner of Christ,
To fight against sin, the world, and the devil."
Pity, O seriously pity the man
Who with bright intellect would waste his time
With all his indifference to Almighty God ;
Let him have pity and peace in his life of darkness,

The little time he has to live for himself—
For, alas! he cannot escape death,
Nor the horrors of life hereafter!
But it may again be naturally asked,
Why tamper with the glorious Law of God?
Why, for pride and foolish fashion's sake,
Does he enter that Holy Church of God
In seeming sanctified nonsense of solemn mockery?
To see and be seen of men—ah! foolish pride :
Alas! his conceited mind of no reasoning power
Is quite sufficient to point him out.
The greatest object of contempt—no, no, pity—
Let him stretch forth his withered hand.
Start not—ah! with heavy sigh—no, no,
For that betrays weakness—ah! yes, he believes,
Or why these signs of horror-grief and dread
Whene'er he hears the name of Death,
Who hath the greatest affection for him.
And, but alas! will ere long grasp him tightly,
For soon he'll be too weary of this short life,
Found wanting and resting on Sorrow's bridge :
Ah! there with dark suspicious look he'll raise his head,
To watch that glimmering—nay, glorious light
Over Mount Calvary—the Star of the East—of the world ;
But his vision, if possible, will be more imperfect
When separated from his righteous brethren
By that Great Gulf which ever divides
Just and good from the abounding wicked.
'Tis only there in everlasting shame
He'll believe in God when—alas! it is too late.

O religion, what treasure to be found !
Do we not look on our endeared friends,
Our father, mother, little children, and think
Of the blessings there are in store for them
In that heavenly world of eternal bliss,
With a merciful, loving, never-dying God ?
Let us learn to pray and then to teach ;
There is this Christian duty incumbent on all :
Train the young to godliness, and advise the aged.
Should we not live in honour and gratitude of each other ?
Does not humility and love constitute a right feeling ?
It is the blessed essence of true religion ;
But whilst there is so much darkness,
" The lovers of cruelty and promoters of misery,
Who have no reverence for God,"
Nor regard, e'en thought, for a fellow-being—
Ah ! there cannot be too much teaching of the Gospel :
O that they will come and hear it,
And be made worthy members of Christ's Church !
The pride and vanity of this world will soon pass away ;
All things must die—are continually dying.
Ah ! whilst we are neglecting our souls,
Or feeding on immortal truth—God's word—
We shall soon die ; but there is this consolation :
On a dying bed the Christian may look up—
Ah ! in his last breathing—and see the Heavens opened ;
The next moment he beholds Jesus at the bedside,
Surrounded by great—ah ! unspeakable glory,
Awaiting to receive him in his bosom.
Ah ! blessed Death, the birthday of immortality !

O let us live and train up our young children,
That *we* may not prevent their going home,
When Christ with unfolded arms bids them come
To that heavenly blessed home of bliss.
O let us look each one to his actions,
And, if possible, regulate them to perfectness ;
So, by continually striving in the Spirit,
We may have grace and blessed freedom—
E'en power divine with God in Christ.
Let us *learn* the way to live and *teach* it !
There is more pleasure in giving than receiving—
That is, in Christian, godly examples,
Because it is love we have for Him.
O let us become the architect of spiritual goodness—
Of our eternal fortune—the wealth of Heaven !

THE DRUNKARD.

DRUNKENNESS ! piteous misery ! what ?
Man forsake his wife and home—sweet home,
For the enticing comforts of an offensive alehouse,
Which ought to be shunn'd as deadly poison ?
But only the drunkard makes it what it is :
By foolish habit he drinks, but drinks to excess,
Till past recovery or amendment—lost for ever
Below the level of the brute—sweet liberty gone.

Ah, but that is not all.
Go !—go to the humble shed of the drunkard :
In the coldest midnight of winter,
Through the broken window that admits the wind and snow,
You'll see the drunkard's wife alone, crouched on straw,
Shivering intensely cold, sorrowfully weeping ;
No fire, no food, no light, but in dark silence
Listening for footsteps—awaiting the return
Of that stern, wild drunkard, whom she loves ;
Pitying, forgiving him ev'ry wicked act,
E'en whilst he regards it sport to make her weep ;
In her bewildered state she blesses him,
Caressing him in love and prayer to God,
That he may yet become a sober man.

Poor woman !
Heaven must be her home for all this sorrow.
Ah, night after night, she's left alone to weep,
Nothing to gladden her heart but the stars above.

Which she attempts to count
One by one. But learn the secret sorrow of her heart,
Ah, troubled mind ! calm sleep of night she ne'er knew.
Her poor weary, almost lifeless frame
Can only hint the sorrowing pain she bears ;
That generous feeling, ah, that grateful fondness
For one who should have been her tenderest friend :
You see it on her brow—you hear it not.
That worthless, wretched drunkard
Is her friend and protector through life. But what ?
He's past recovery. By drink he is driven mad.

E

And his poor wife to an untimely grave.
A profitable lesson this—ah, it may be learned
By the drunkard, to whom we give advice,
Not fearing the truth because it seems so hard.

                    It may be said
We see our brothers' faults, but not our own ;
We judge of them whilst they find fault with us ;
It may be that we are not quite sober ;
Sober-minded, or why judge we of others ?
Ah, perhaps the world is mad, and we're all insane ;
If so, the beam that's in the eye hath made the mischief.

                    But are we mad ?
Living without sincerity, love, and truth,
Mistrusting each other and bitterly contending
Who is to be the master or the patient,
For now each claims to be his brother's keeper.
But how few there are who care to give advice ;
Perhaps no one capable of receiving it.
But why is this ? Ah, because we know too well
We freely offer that which costs us nothing,
Which makes it rare to find a friend sincere,
Because there is no charity.

                    But what is life ?
Ah, life, indeed, is full of personal wrongs ;
But the clear-headed, sober man
May look at things honestly as they are.
Alas ! when his mind becomes intoxicated
By the poisonous drink that's freely offered,

Just to poison the mind of a fellow-creature,
That which once pleased him may become now displeasing.
But the very wicked have their friends to love,
And what is poison to one is balm to another,
As we take the one-sided view of each other;
Whilst envy and hatred smile to deceive us all—
Hence the world's many changing sorrows.

GOOD FRIDAY.

Look on Him but once more—
That sacrifice of truth.   Oh ! see
Him now upon the accursed tree,
Suff'ring but to set us free—
His agony deplore !

That bitter cup, ah, stifling breath,
Hast'ning on the hour of death :
" It is finished now," He saith :
Alas ! He is no more.

For us He only lived to die ;
Behold His dreadful majesty :
Is such not life's great mystery ?
Behold Him now once more !

EASTER-DAY.

WEEP not, why weep ?
The Lord's awaken'd out of sleep ;
Refresh'd. Behold His loving glance,
   Whilst He points to life above,
On His smiling countenance,
   Exulting in His Father's love :
Oh, what thrilling joy is given
In the light and truth of Heaven !

THE OLD YEAR GONE !

ADIEU, Old Year, thou'st no returning day—
   Gone for ever : thy parting moments blest,
As in a dream of glory pass'd away
   In silence and in harmony for rest.
Gone for ever ; yet thy memory dear
   Shall cheer the heart, e'en death's consoling power
Can sweeten hope in Nature's mortal hour,
   'Tho' all things die, and time will soon be o'er.

Farewell, Old Year, thou'st no returning day,
   In quietude thou'rt hushed to sleep and rest ;
Thy trembling form in death hath pass'd away,
   And in the New Year's glory thou art blest.

TYRANNICAL PRIDE.

By care much trouble's always found—
    Indeed 'tis never lost,
To him who weeds the barren ground
    At other people's cost.
But what of pride, that sick'ning pride ?
Oh, who would be the wretch supplied
With tinsel crown ?—ah ! scorn to bear,
For having such a toy so rare ;
The ornament can well express
The language of its own success,
Better far than truth can guess.
The very thought distracts the brain,
And gives humiliating pain.
Oh, what an everlasting shame,
        By second birth
        To gain such worth !
For empty pride to lose a name,
In bondage thus to live again !
Ah ! such undaunted hope inclined
Can only show the state of mind.

WHY CAST DOWN ?

That Physician of mind, where is He, my lad ?
    Why in sorrowing dread so cast down ?
Hast thou called for His help?—come speak, oh, why sad ?
    Confess where is hope—look around.

Consolation canst thou take, or spiritual food?
   Where is faith? oh, look up and take heed;
To evil all are prone, but love whispers good,
   And th' heav'nly Physician all need.

But why in such trouble? oh, sorrowing soul;
   Live, learn of good charity's creed;
Give all that thou hast, and the mind shall control,
   Secret joy of the poor thou shalt feed.

A letter from God (hast thou broken the seal?),
   Containing the truth of His light:
Mark well the contents—His med'cine will heal,
   And establish thy health to delight.

The soul thus new-born shall live in His trust,
   The body though holy shall be,
Altho' soon, alas! to crumble to dust,
   Yet the soul shall be happy and free
   In the light of eternity.

ANGELS WITHOUT WINGS.

        In spite of living strife,
Angel-woman lives to comfort man:
   To cheer him, as it were, to joys above.
By sympathetic tenderness she can
   Fill the world with quenchless glowing love
Angel-like in virtue but to shine,
   More of Heav'n than earth uprais'd and given
To smile in beauty full of grace divine,
   To live and love, and guide man safe to Heaven.

THE SLEEPING INFANT.

LIFE in death—ah, light of power and glory,
Behold the Lamb ; behold the child of God !
Behold innocence—ah, pale and cold in death,
As in a joyous dream to awake again
In glory of its Maker.   That solemn sleep,
That heav'n-like countenance, calm repose
That truth upon its brow, that loving smile,
Impressed by God.   Behold the Lamb—the child !
Such innocence and beauty can alone
Belong to Him, in silent praise of glory,
Betokening the presence of its Maker.
Behold the hand of Him whose pitying care,
Whose loving touch of power-working joy
Has changed that earthly form for life in Him,
Changed for peaceful rest and holy love,
In Paradise to dwell.   Behold the child !
Yea, " for of such is the kingdom of Heaven."
But behold thy God—look up in joy and love.
O worship Him continually, worship Him
In faith and truth ; yea, as a little child
Of loving tenderness and smiling hope.
Ah, life in death, the soul for ever lives.
O can we live and not be thankful to Him,
The great Creator God of light and life ?

THE LANGUAGE OF LOVE.

"There is within the world in which we dwell
A friendship answering to the world full well ;
An interchange of looks and actions kind,
And in some sense an interchange of mind :"
Which confidence gives in truth of love
To uplift the heart to sacred joys above.
For, mark the light upon the angel-face—
What holy beauty, innocence, we trace ;
The purity of righteousness and grace ;
Engaging love, the highest virtue given,
Whilst language of the eye speaks but of Heaven ;
That harmonizing bliss of light above,
Which is of God, for God himself is Love.

WEEDS.

In number endless, in construction perfect, exquisitely
    beautiful
Are these small gems, flow'ry weeds, which voluntarily
    spring forth
To amuse, instruct, and to give man labour, undoubtedly
    to benefit him.
Silently, yet how solemnly they speak the admiration of
    the Deity,
Full of language, and as wonderful to behold as the most
    lovely flowers

Possessed as they are of innumerable worlds in bright
array,
Of countless millions of minute animated beings
Apparently full of joy, serving the living God in magnified
wisdom.
Ah! man, indeed, may very seriously consider his de-
fective vision—
This consummate skill, power, and heavenly wisdom,
e'en in that which he disdains.

May 2nd, 1861.

"LITTLE CHILDREN, LOVE ONE ANOTHER."

LITTLE children, learn to pray,
And His holy laws obey.
Time will soon have passed away ;
'Tis morn, 'tis noon—alas! the day
   Too soon is spent ! Oh do not say
   Ye have no time ; begin
   To lisp the first short prayer to Him,
   With heart and voice His praises sing ;
Your Father's love true joy shall bring,
And power to love each other.   Fear
God and do your duty here,
In little kindnesses to cheer
   The hearts that should be loved and dear—
   Kind words are sweet to Angels' ear,
   While Love and Charity are near
   To wipe away the falling tear.

Loving-kindness soothes the heart,
Heals the spirit's cruel smart.
Little ones ! do each your part,
Love each other while you may,
For all, like flowers that bloom to-day,
Must die and moulder in decay
Till dawns the final Judgment Day.

NO TIME FOR TRIFLING HERE.

BEHOLD the bier !
How suddenly do disappear
Friends and foes.   Alas ! I fear
There is no time for trifling here.
                    Think of this.

See the dead, but once robust,
Now a senseless heap of dust.
Ha, alas ! too soon we must,
                    Think of this,

Part from ev'ry worldly friend,
This melancholy life to end—
Look up, to holiness attend.
                    Think of this.

Why cast down, with weeping eye ?
In pray'r He can lift us high
Where the soul can never die.
                    Think of this.

Rich and poor, one and all,
Only waiting for His call,
Soon in death, alas ! to fall.

> Think of this.

Let the foolish vain be brave,
Little time his soul to save—
No repentance in the grave.

> Think of this.

———◆———

FRIENDSHIP.

THE friendship of the good and wise
Creates a charm that never dies,
   But strengthens men to give
Their confidence, returning love,
Doing His good will above
   The little time they live.

More precious far than worlds of gold
Is that kind heart that's never cold ;
   Sincere, ay, always true :
Cheering us through life's rough storm,
And all deceitful dealings scorn,
   Whilst giving each his due.
   Alas ! such friends are few.

No wonder then his joys we share,
We feel his grief, his sorrows bear,
And breathe to God our earnest prayer

To bless him from above.
But while the tear-drop's on the cheek
For one so gentle, kind and meek,
The heart gives more than tongues can speak ;—
Real sentiments of love.

March 20*th*, 1868.

THE GLOW-WORM, THE MOLE, AND THE EARTHWORM.

Thou black
Mysterious worm, why show thy light—
    Simply for a lark ?
To blind one quite who has no sight
    Unless 'tis in the dark ?
Go, burrow in the earth to rise,
There dig thy way up to the skies—
Be off ! fly, fly !   The glow-worm knew
    Moles should not come to light,
To look above, or to review
    What can give no delight.
" Ha, ha !" says mole, " my useful eyes
    Find all things bright, you know :
A Paradise of loving ties,
    Where light can never show
    The joy of wealth below ;
Where earthworms never can surprise,
    Tho' harmless without stings ;
Above the earth, yea, to the skies,
    They'd rise if they had wings."

THE IDLE NEWSMONGER.

WE recollect him when a boy,
  How fond he was of play,
And how he cried for every toy
  That fell into his way.

But now that time has gone, and he
  Has pass'd his prime, I ween,
Although he's little wiser now
  Than when a youngster seen.

He trots along from house to house.
  Each neighbour to abuse,
But to be rid of such a cure
  They start him off with news.

The future news gives him that pride
  To keep up childish games ;
You'll always find him side by side
  Among the tattling dames.

August 3rd, 1870.

WEEDS AND FLOWERS.

THE worthiest of men,
  Of judgment and reason,
May sometimes disown
  A flower out of season.

Why should one mistake
    A weed for a flower
Of transforming beauty,
    In glory and power?
Go ask the wise critic,
    Of unclouded mind,
For such nice distinction
    One's troubled to find.
But where is the diff'rence,
    When two "stars" shall shine
Of unearthly beauty,
    And both so divine?
In this generation,
    Unnoticed may grow
Small flowers of creation,
    Undistinguished, you know:
Whilst weeds may attract
    For their beauty in bloom,
Microscopically seen,
    Just for taking up room.
Why magnify weeds
    To such glorious power,
In size and in beauty
    Surpassing the flower?
Small weeds that grow high,
    Despised, ay, what spirit;
Yet why should they die,
    For such singular merit?
But ah, such is life.

Do weeds not display
The wisdom of God?
For who dares to say
The light of His wisdom
They do not convey?
His teaching is glory,
The truth of creation ;
They come uninvited,
So humble in station ;
But the Hand that hath made them
Created alike
The weed and the flower
By the touch of His light.
Then let us examine
Small weeds that invite,
Our sympathy cheer,
For they have a right
To live and rejoice
In the light that is given,
To glory and praise
Their Maker of Heaven.
Cut them up, ay, alas !
Whilst they flourish to shade
The uncared-for insect
For which they were made.
Let man then reflect,
Oh ignorant race,
To see in their glory
His light they may trace :

Great wisdom display'd
  In weeds they despised.
There's nothing misplac'd—
  In the "stars" that arise,
Through Him the great God,
  In whom we have light
To notice the humble,
  And to cheer in delight
The weed or the flower
  He delights to call forth,
To live but an hour,
  Or to die in their birth.
Why should we misuse
  The power that is given?
Why live to abuse
That which should amuse,
And teach us to gain,
His mercy obtain,
The wisdom of Heaven?

COME, JOYOUS YEAR.

COME, joyous year, and bring new pleasures;
  Chase away the winter cold;
The glory of thy passing treasures
  Let fall upon the young and old.

Let honesty and truth in part
    Warm all hearts with aims most pure,
Love and friendship to impart,
    Their swelling joys all to allure.
Feed the hungry, that no tear
May be dropped throughout the year.

THE FOP.

                Oh, odious sight !
The foplin's crowned with burnished gold,
    As costly as his rings ;
His stars, real diamonds, pins, untold,
    Each precious jewel brings
    Pleasure without stings
    To give the " blazer " wings;
For greater honours to produce
A grand display, the proper use
    Exhaling scents to please ;
By mixed perfumes, a sure resource,
The new-made Stilton to enforce
Real blessings, but of course
    The blockhead must demand his fees
    Ere the taster's in his cheese ;
He'll find, alas ! the secret's out,
'Twill give him room to strut about
    A wiser, greater fool.   Oh, no !
    The perfect fopling's made for show,
    To please the ignorant here below.

F

THE FIERY LADY OF ATTRACTION.

ONE would suppose
Her red-tipp'd nose,
And scorching cheeks, were in a blaze ;
Her eyes a glaring fire ;
But whilst we on her glory gaze,
And almost melted in the rays,
Her tongue would never tire.

Her waspish figure, half in two,
The Grecian bend high soaring ;
The clumsy heel and tiny shoe,
Show but the beauty of the screw
To set us off a roaring.

The slightest glance at her would thrill
The heart, to set us sighing ;—
But there, 'tis no use crying :
We must succumb, if 'tis her will
To show politeness, and with skill
Our cheerfulness in dying.

August 5th, 1870.

THE " SWELL " OF THE PERIOD.

TURN not the scornful look, nor hiss aloud
The puffed-up " swell," vain, and with joy elate,
Whose real success can only make him proud ;
But rather fill his empty-headed pate.

So by degrees he'll swell to burst with joys,
    ('To emulate the "little imps" around,
And spill his dirty water on the ground)
    Ne'er again to rise to make a noise.

" DEAD, INOPERATIVE, UNINFLUENCING NOTION."

A WARNING.

YE earth-born proud, why thus invade—
    The devil's rights enforce ?
Shall we not give our warning aid
    On the rugged path of course ?
Alas, proud dust, a "star" so great,
    Who made you what you are ?
To seek for power in Church and State,
    When the heart, alas ! is far
From Him who called us forth in love
    To teach and preach below,
And show the way to Him above,
    Where the poorest hope to go.
Why make long prayers with men of strife,*
    Who seek the loaves and fishes,
To forfeit joy-eternal life ?—
    What most a glutton wishes
    Is the clatter of his dishes

* Luke xxii. 24.

F 2

And jingling of ill-gotten wealth,
   To him 'tis life and breath ;
To intoxicate the mind, such pelf
   Shall purchase pain and death.
Ha ! thirty pieces bought our God,
   Jesus Christ, we know—
   But such is life below.
The childish toys beneath the sod,
   Where quacks dress up for show,
   Ambition's spark to glow :
Such fools contend for wealth to sway,
   They seek the highest place,*
'Till one by one Death takes away
   To triumph in disgrace.
How few would preach were they not paid ?
   For whilst they live in part,
They seek the sun—but in the shade—
   To warm each dark cold heart.
Angels of light, mark where ye tread,
   To uplift the poor from pain,
Smite not the living counted dead
   Who search below for gain.
Good God ! bless both the rich and poor
   Who live to love each other !
Ope wide the mansion, cottage door—
Give them Thy light for evermore
   Who welcomes in a brother.
Yea, their reward shall come at last—

* Luke xx. 46, 47.

Thou knowest, God, the heart
Of man.   Is Time not flying fast,
And soon with Thee they'll meet to part
   No more, in joy that's given
   In light-eternal Heaven?

Forgive the proud, oh God, forgive !
   Let Thy imperial sway
Teach men to serve Thee whilst they live,
   And glorify their day—
Of humble prayer, devoted breath,
   Before they pass away :
Have pity in the hour of death
   Who would Thy laws obey.

A few short days and we are gone,
   Forgotten here below,
The night's far spent, and soon the morn
   Will bring to light the foe.
All those who live for gain—but woe
   To those who curse the poor :
The headstrong proud may war, we know,
   Outside the heavenly door,
And cry at last—Lord, Lord, arise !
   The ignorant wise in state,
Open the door, their weeping eyes.
"I know you not."   Alas ! their sighs
   And prayers have come too late.

Good, glorious God, teach us to live—
  Oh punish not the wrong !
But give us holy light to live
  And bless Thee in our song—
  Alas ! our time's not long.

Behold in Nature, mark the change,
  Friends and foes depart.
Thy holy law, how wondrous strange ! —
  Oh change, oh change the heart
Of one and all, great God of love,
  To whom Thou'st given breath ;
Give all eternal joy above
  When we depart in death.

These lines be understood aright,
  Altho' perchance, I fear,
The one who has but little light,
  His foot-notes make him clear.

JOYFUL NEWS.

FRAGMENT.

O SOUL-REVIVING feast,
Behold the brightness of that glorious star,
In holiness beyond this world afar,
    Arising in the East
To cheer us, and to lead us in the way
Of light and truth on Holy Christmas Day !

Sound forth the bells—tell the joyful news
   Throughout the world in joy-exulting breath,
  Glad tidings of a Saviour. None refuse
   To make it known—He comes to conquer death,
      And set us free
      To all eternity.

NATURE'S PRAISE.

    UNGRATEFUL man! doth not
Nature smile to praise her God? and who
  Can watch her now unfold th' expanding flower
Without that genial hope to serve Him too
  In holiness, through his short passing hour?
Great men of intellect, as they survey
  The wondrous beauties springing from the sod,
To teach the world there is a silent way
  To glorify the all-wise living God,
Must be convinced. He who endowed the mind
  Would have all men seek truth from Him above,
Live in peace, be gentle, good and kind,
  And dwell upon His joy-redeeming love,
  In living light from the bright realms above.
    Behold her beauties! see what Nature's given
      To raise poor fallen man! Alas! to-day
    She smiles His praise and points the way to Heaven:
      To-morrow (oh, man's care!)—who then shall say?
    All her glory shall have passed away.

Fast fly the moments—(oh the wicked heart
   To be unkind, and just for self to live !)
Too soon, alas ! our injured friends depart :—
   Could we recall them, oh, what would we give !
Reflect, alas ! ye proud, frail mortal dust,
   And learn to live as you would live for Heaven.
Whilst Nature smiles to praise her God of light,
   The meanest object has His care and love.
Shall we not, then, adore Him in delight ?
   What is frail man that he should live above,
Whilst here below he knows not what is right ?
   No gratitude for e'en life that's given,
   How can he hope to make his way to Heaven ?

BEAUTY IN ALL THINGS.

There's beauty in the morning,
   Passing on in light,
Fleeting life adorning,
   Seeking rest at night.

In time advancing duty
   All must pass away,
To find unchanging beauty
   Of never-ending day.

There's beauty in the night,
   When stars are fixed for ever,
To smile in holy light
   And glorify their Giver.

There's beauty e'en in death,
   When holier joys await,
To give eternal breath
   Which love and light create.

For God is light and love,
   And He alone can give
Eternal life above,
   Where saints and angels live.

REFLECTIONS ON THE GLORIOUS MONUMENTS OF CANTERBURY CATHEDRAL.

AMONG the stately monuments,
Deep in thought, whilst musing on the past,
We seem to lose ourselves in dizzy dream,
Amid the grandeur of this hallowed place
Of holy wonders of admired beauty :
The honoured tributes of departed worth,
The glorious trophies of the brave and good,
Whose wondrous deeds inscribed, alas ! that we
May sing their praises whilst they shine above
In living glory as the stars of Heaven.

July, 1867.

"THAT WE SHOULD PRAY FOR OUR MINISTERS."

THE Holy Spirit dictates the Father's will,
And so revives with living care divine
The sacred soul to holiness and love,
That man may have the pow'r to teach His word.
    O, what glowing heartfelt joy indeed,
When the soul becomes awakened by the light
Of glorious Christianity !
    In faith and love,
    In science of happiness,
    And in the study of virtue,
The loving Shepherd feeds His little flock
In the spacious field of wisdom's
Cultivated living light and glory,
On hidden manna sent direct from God.
    The poor wanderer, destitute and cold,
Finds his welcome in His pitying smile
Of holy tenderness and sacred love :—
    O God be praised !
Then for our ministers should we not pray,
Whose high privilege is to instruct a brother,
E'en to the salvation of his soul ?
    And O, that thine holy influence
May kindle within us that spiritual love
Of holy truth divine they seek to give,
By the help of God, in glory of His kingdom's
Harmonizing power—eternal light
Of heavenly smiling joy.

CHARITY.

CHARITY,
  Blest angel of our land,
She lives to do His will above,
To cherish, ah, in secret love,
  What gifts in her right hand.

  To the humble cottage door
She seeks the suff'ring ones—her own,
Or wherein distress is known,
  To help the downcast poor.

  What hearts does she not move,
Whilst with the lowly she appears,
With gifts to drain away their tears
  In holiness of love?

  God's light is on her face,
Whilst among the afflicted poor,
To comfort, cheer each dreary hour
  In smiles of living grace.

THE FALSE STEP.

IN the slow step of gradual decay
Hope tells us of glorious things to come,
Whilst Faith in love-like meekness leads us through
The avenues of Wisdom's beauteous,
Eternal, holy smiles of Light and Truth.

Oh ! but alas !
Before we reach that region of joy
Obtrusive Vanity stops us by the way
To entice us with fascinating smiles,
To glorify His name in foolish pride,
Ensnaring us with false, expiring praise,
Till we forget our God—mistake the path
Which leads to that eternal home of bliss,
And by one deviating step we're found
Journeying in the by-road of sorrow—
Lost for ever in the shadow of sin,
Ah ! fetter'd by darkness in our tott'ring age.

THE ANGEL-TEACHER.

FRAGMENT.

In righteousness,
Rejecting the world,
  Ha ! to live for another ;
Imparting the truth
  To save a poor brother ;
Children around thee,
  In faith that is given,
Learning to sing
  The sweet love-song of Heaven,
Whilst hoping for peace,
  Enshrouded in light,
Watching and waiting
  For the land of delight—

(O glory divine, divine !)
    Of life-giving rest ;
Breathing a prayer
    That all may be blest :
Thou teacher of good,
    E'er smiling to cheer,
By life-giving love,
    The little ones near :
Hail, virtuous one !
    Of life-smiling love,
Rejecting the world,
    For joys far above ;
Glory and honour
    Show the light given—
Honour and glory
    Await thee in Heaven.

July 25th, 1870.

BABES OF THE PERIOD.

OVERGROWN babes would always try
    To step it, if they could but walk—
Bless their little hearts, how shy !
    Seldom do they learn to talk :
See them crawl to get a look
Perhaps at some large picture-book :
    The rattle and the ring aside,
    What can such ones know of pride ?

For see their playthings in a heap,
'Tis enough to make one weep,
Were it not that toys are cheap ;
    And good useful knowledge flowing.
    Darling boobies, puffing, blowing,
    Losing rattle, capering, crowing—
    Ah, but see their looks, how knowing !
They're sure to find it in their sleep.

July 23rd, 1870.

TO A CHILD THAT DIED AS SOON AS IT WAS BORN.

God sent thee, little one, on earth,
    But not to see this light,
And yet the glory of thy birth
    Was heav'nly, pure delight.
Hush'd to sleep in godly joy,
    And taken up on high
To live in love and joyous light
    With Him beyond the sky.
No sinful stains upon thy heart—
    Celestial power divine
Bid thee to come and thence depart
    In glory-light to shine.
But who would wish to see thee live ?
    That inborn glory tells
Us of that peace and joy within
    Where light for ever dwells.

No earthly power can dim that light
  Which comes direct from God,
For by the glory of delight
  'Tis guided by His rod.
Then, smiling infant, sleep on—sleep,
  No earthly sins to dread ;
The evil spirit cannot peep
Into the mysteries, oh ! so deep.
  To touch the living dead :
Gone for ever, far above,
  To live in light, to shine
In the arms of living Love
  And smiling power divine.

FAITH.

Unseen by mortal eye,
On bended knee in secret prayer,
  The child drew forth a sigh,
In longing holy love to be
  With Jesu up on high.

That little one so full of grace—
  How holy faith like this
Reflects the image of His face
  To prove his godliness !
Jesu heard the prayerful sigh ;
The little one's prepared to die.
  In crowning happiness.

SHORTNESS OF LIFE.

THE sun's declining,
And time, alas ! is passing at full speed
    To show that life is but a dying hour.
Oh, mark the change ! and watch from whence proceeds
    His dispensation ! Oh, mysterious power !
Lo, ere another day we may be gone :—
    Shall we, then, take our leave of ev'ry friend
Just for the night ? Maybe, before the morn
    They, too, in their mortality may find their end.

THE POSTMAN'S SABBATH.

LET the man of letters rest
    From his labours once a week,
That his Sunday may be blest :
    In that light should we not seek
To help him spend that glorious day
    (In holiness lowly, meek,
Before Him), ere he pass away
    To face us at the Judgment Day ?

August 28*th*, 1870.

A CURSE.

MAY he who would by snares entrap
A poor unguarded child of love
Find neither sleep of rest, nor friends
In sorrow, curs'd until life ends,
As retribution from above!

September 1st, 1870.

THE CALL OF JESU.

THE lame shall walk ;
By His light the blind shall see,
And feel their great Redeemer's love.
But hark ! He's calling me and thee :
" Come ye weary unto Me,
And refresh yourselves above,
At the marriage feast of love."
See Him beckon hither, see
That smiling look of loving care,
Whilst He listens to our pray'r,
Bidding every soul beware
Not to lose the sight of Him
In the morn or evening hymn,
That all should His glory share
By that holy constant prayer,
In His light that sets us free
To joyous life eternity.

LAUGHING-STOCKS.

THERE are so many rising " stars " of fame
That critics know not whom to praise or blame,
Whilst envious doctors live to disagree,
And prove their powers by an high degree :
Professors all may simply live to cheer,
But then success depends on their small-beer—
The boozy-headed sure to grasp for all,
Blest England's " stars," how many live to fall,
To rise again, perchance, in better grace.
Ha ha ! if so, there can be no disgrace.

How many strut about in borrowed plumes,
To build their glory e'en amongst the tombs ;
But that we leave of course : we want the grace
And powers to show the wisdom of our race.
In every trade the " dealer's " skill we find—
Not one in wisdom-skill is thought behind.
The " duffer " with his " 'normous " sacrifice,
For less than half he sells his goods—to rise ;
To make a fortune by his cunning lies.
Sly as a fox, the scheming, learned quack
Will cringe, and fawn, and oft make white look black :
These " over-fed " poor sick, both lame and blind,
Pretend they're good, tho' virtue never find ;
Good-natur'd drones, see how they lag behind.

We turn to self, another truth to find :
Not one of us is living without sin.
A tinkling trap may please the ignorant hind,
The sounding bell will prove it's not all tin ;

The "doctor" goes to church like other men,
But in feigned duty, ere the prayers begin,
He bids his servant call him out again.
Some advertise themselves by coming late,
And leave their seat just to avoid the plate,
And oft disturb their friends of eager musing ;
An awful thing, of course, to contemplate—
The House of God, His power and law abusing.

The giant man who has but little brain
Is courted for his wealth ; then why complain ?
The dress'd-up body—ignorance and gold—
Cannot give youthful bloom to one that's old.
Is such then life ?   Ha, preachers teach in vain,
The wildest black sheep they can never tame ;
These human monsters have of course no shame,
Whilst they intent pursue their mundane aim—
The worldly riches, just for sinful gain.
How many " Jacks," false prophets of our day,
Who care not what they do nor what they say !

Poor hypocrites ! they preach of His salvation,
Deny their God in light of His creation :
The golden calf, alas ! how many crave
To carry riches simply to the grave !
Such cupidous pretenders only prove,
For any meanness they would make a move.
How many skilful " riders " in the race
Get thrown ! some, too, pick'd up in sad disgrace :
To show how much they need the doctor's skill,
They take his mixtures oft against their will.
Let courage still sustain such men of force.
The high-bred may be " wanting " in the course

VULGARITY.

" E'EN little fleas have lesser fleas
     Upon their backs to bite 'em ;
And these, again, have lesser fleas ;
     And so, *ad infinitum*."
The sultry weather does, no doubt,
Surely bring the " *warmint* " out,
     And other biting ticklish things :
The pest'ring gnats that fly about,
     With lazy drones that have no stings,
     Could do no harm had they no wings
To rise on high and buzz about,
     To show importance here below,
     As rich-dress'd butterflies for show.
But such is life, alas ! we dwell
     'Mongst senseless jades of blissful fame
So grand, ah, ah, but who can tell ?
     They've neither character nor name ;
     But then great " larning " hides their shame.
On barren land they turn, no doubt,
To show the tongue is always out,
Demoralizing—life's a " sell,"
Where great and small frogs croak and swell
To show there is a common hell,
Where the evil demon fell,
When the virtuous every hour
Overstep to show their power.

"MAKING HAY WHILE THE SUN SHINES."

" THE wandering poet takes his tithe
Of music from the sweeping scythe,
Or merry maidens laughing blithe
      In love's sweet way."

Not e'en an action can be mean
In rural sports upon the green ;
How many little ones are seen,
Each smiling, dancing, fairy queen,
      So full of play.

Children's little help well done,
Their nurses, too, join in the fun
With eager glances ; see them run
Their flying colours in the sun,
      New on to-day.

What transport joys—ha ! who could scold
The noisiest of the young or old ?
How many tender buds unfold
To prove that love is never cold
      In life's sun-ray !

Forgetful almost of the past,
Ha ! whilst the moments fly so fast,
Oh may no idle dream o'ercast
When e'en such pleasures shall have past
      Beyond the day !

O happy little child of song,
Skipping age amid the throng,
Bless its little heart ! how long
Will it keep itself from wrong
        Whilst making hay ?

AUTUMN.

"THERE IS A FEARFUL SPIRIT BUSY NOW !"

        THE grape-like
Clust'ring hops hang from the poles
    (Blest harvest of the poor) ;
The russet leaf shall we misname ?
Time and Nature now acclaim
God's holy will but to maintain,
Whilst dreary winter's selfish aim
    Is plighted death once more.
Is man too languid now to rise
    And thank his God in pray'r,
For all the glories 'neath the skies
    Consign'd to winter's care ?
Flowers, alas ! why cease to bloom ?
    E'en Nature seems to say ;
The garden-fields and woods too soon
    Foretell of their decay,
    God's law but to obey.

Have we no hope? Will spring return
  To give life-cheering hour,
  Tho' th' earthly stars of pow'r
Soon fade in death? Will man not learn?
God's secret hand can he discern?
And live in hope but for return
  The smiling, budding flower?
But light has fled, and man complains,
  No hope—a cloudy day:
Ha, Death must smile when winter reigns,
  Earth's beauties must decay.
How soon the change, alas! how soon!
E'en th' grasshopper hath changed his tune,
  The cricket and the crow
  Are silent now, alas! 'tis so;
  Soon the cutting winds will blow,
    Flowers and plants soon gone;
  Or buried 'neath the winter's snow,
  To sleep and rest in smiles we know,
    To awake the coming morn.
O transport joy, returning day,
The flowers we dreamt had pass'd away
  Will surely come again, His care:
  Let man, then, hope in watchful pray'r,
His unchanging laws obey,
Till the coming Judgment Day.

THE ADMIRING BEAUTIES OF THE WOOD.

No archer am I,
And yet, by-the-by,
I'd be " monarch of all I survey "—
    Tall trees of harmonious speech.
Yea, I would listen to ev'ry lay ;
The songs, rustic notes by-the-way,
    The glorious reproaches they teach.
Were I lord of the vine or the rose,
    The fig or the unkindly thorn,
I should soon cut them up, I suppose,
    The oak, maple, yew, to adorn.
Yea, I'd cut them into veneer,
    To polish and give a new face ;
Would unite both the green and the sere—
    Not one of them would I misplace—
The alder, the larch, but again
    The ebony and holly may frown
Because they've no tint ; ay, but then
    Not for colour alone I cut down.
To me the cork's bark is no good,
    Nor the produce of wondrous pine ;
Yet I glory to cut up the wood,
    'Tho' the bark I reject as divine.
The apple, the pear, or the plum,
    I value their wood more than fruit ;
But do I despise the last one,
    Tho' the thorn may prick sometimes a brute,
    Yet " my rights there is none to dispute."

BUILDING A TOMB.

PRAY what's the use of tyrants being brave?
   Birth, rank, and wealth, all things below,
Find not the slightest honour in the grave;
   Nor can they elevate the soul; we know
How many only live to build a tomb
   By the worldly pleasures they have bought,
Then pass away into oblivion gloom,
   To moulder and decay, a thing of nought,
Dead to God, alas!—to future light.

MAN, THE ARCHITECT OF HIS OWN FORTUNE; OR,

LIFE'S LABOUR LOST.

A FABLE.

LIFE'S labour lost!
See that poor snail—a pilgrim on the road—
   Can scarcely crawl to thus endure his gloom;
His house upon his back, but what a load!
   Convincing proof how much he loves his home
   To go abroad to show his moving tomb;
And thus create e'en envy to conspire.
The meanest slug comes up e'en from the mire
To build his temple without light inspire.
The smallest worm perchance may see the spire
Without a chance of rising any higher;
The ladybird may cheer the warm report,

The ant may praise, the critic spider snub
Such architects for grovelling in the dirt,
     But what can be expected from a grub?
Let man now stoop and learn of life to know
The wealth and glory of small things below.
A Paradise of diamonds there unfold,
An honest measure of rich flowing gold;
There tiptoe mountebanks can cheer each other
     'Mongst bits of coffin-lids and human bones;
For down below they recognise a brother
     Whilst excavating 'neath the senseless stones
In search of stars below the roots of grass
For wealth where only worms can dwell, alas!
To ask of rotten bones for light to pass
     Above the heads of flowers where great men walk;
     And many a fruitless quack is paid to talk
About the gold and costly gems they know
Among the dead men's bones they seek below.

All learned quacks go down to build below,
Then emigrate above to make a show.
     Fantastic fools of little minds, alas!
     Are dang'rous as the snake that's in the grass,
     We meditate their landmark as we pass.
Far down below their heads they carry high—
Begin to live when they're about to die.

THE NIGHTINGALE AND THE WORM.

WITH eye so full of light
The early bird may "pick up" by his skill
  The undefended worm that crawls the earth,
But what advantage would it be to kill
  A grovelling family of untimely birth ?
How many giants, ay, that are rough shod !
  But birds and insects have unequal power :
The largest worm that lies beneath the sod
  Cannot crawl forth to view the smallest flower
But that he meets his enemy on wing
To be swallowed up alive, alas ! poor thing.

LULLABY.

IT snows ; 'tis night ;
The stars are twinkling in the skies,
  To watch o'er thee, ah, in thy sleep !
Then, little darling, close thine eyes,
To find in dream-land some new prize—
  . The winter gone, and rose-buds peep,
To vanish soon as thou shalt wake
To find reality's mistake—
  Snow on the ground e'en six feet deep !

January 15th, 1867.

THE GRASSHOPPER.

HARK, the grasshopper-poet, what joy may he bring,
  His powerful notes so enchanting ;
Attracting small insects too busy to sing,
  Or to join in the song he's now chanting.

The ants and the bees seem to listen in dread,
And justify censure for his being well-bred ;
But listen—attention ! how cuttingly sharp
  Does he stir up the soul to awake :
Such a glorious songster only sings in the dark,
  Just to make my poor heart and head ache.

Not so, ay, alas ! though he makes the head wring ;
Blest grasshopper-poet, long live such a king !
  To wound the refined it seems hard,
Who put on a very wry face when they sing,
  Just to drown the sharp notes of the bard.

Perplex'd and dismay'd, what a tyrant of crime !
  What a keen cutting noise—but what skill !
Such negative graces of joy-killing rhyme,
  To enter the soul like a sharp-pointed drill,
  Is enough to make any light-headed bard ill.

Alas ! but why grieve ? and what's the use sighing ?
  He sings to give life and to save ;
His sharp cutting notes will prevent one from dying
  When he desires to sleep in his grave.

Whilst the ladybird angel is high on the wing,
  And the gods all applaud such a scold ;
To inspire the small grasshopper-poet to sing
  To the rich, poor, the young and the old.

Blest grasshopper-poet, sing on with delight,
  The sun shall smile on thee by day ;
The moon and the stars watch o'er thee at night,
  Whilst we listen to thy nocturnal lay.

THOUGHTS ON DEATH.

DAY by day, yea, ev'ry hour,
The smiling bloom of ev'ry flower
Undergoes a change for death.
So we decline, soon lose our breath—
But ah ! th' immortal spirit lives,
Blest in joy by Him who gives
To man his living light on high,
And bids him now prepare to die.
Though in the dark and silent tomb
All appears so cold and gloom,
Ha ! there they lie, our friends of love,
In dust. Their living souls above
Smile to see us weep, and keep
Watch o'er them whilst they seem to sleep,
Mould'ring in their earthly clay ;
But from the grave they've pass'd away ;
From death to life of joy that's given—
Who would not die to live for Heaven ?

June 14th, 1865.

THE GENIUS AND POWERS OF THE PRESS.

THE *Post* has found his weight in letters,
    The *Star* finds power in light,
Whilst *Punch* of course might show his betters,
    The *Press* can force delight.
The *Dover Telegraph*, we say,
    Need send no news by new *Express :*
And yet the *London News* would pay
Even the *Leader* to convey
The *Spectator* by railway.
The *Critic* has his equal laws,
    May characterise or pun ;
But then the *Guardian* has his cause,
    His common course to run,
    Perhaps to outprise the *Sun*,
    What wit and humour is in *Fun .'*
The *Examiner* in mysteries dive ;
    But just to keep the *Times* alive,
The *Church and State* impart display :
    Bell's Life oft jars " Hark-Hark-away !"
    What hunting, ay, what busy skill,
    How many pop-guns, oh, to fill,
    And yet we find no game to kill ;
    Little to please, and much to vex,
    Love and murder to perplex.
But what of keen *Observer !*
        Kent Herald displays
        Gazette essays ;
    So the *Chronicle* at Dover,
    All do advance intelligence—

Refined in taste and learning :
Open your eyes, there's many a prize
To pay one for discerning.
Long live the *Press* to give delight !
How many little stars of light.
So full of wise invention—
One or two we'll mention :
The *Statesman* in a maze,
Court Journal and the *Engineer*,
The *Law Times* and *Enquirer*.
The *Economist* of praise,
The *Jewish Chronicle*, *John Bull*,
The *Lady's Newspaper* so full,
We wonder how it pays.
The *Atlas* and the *Globe* is seen,
Public Opinion spends his spleen,
Ha, ha, so many ways ;
The *Builder* has a mind,
The *Christian Times*,
Enquirer, sometimes
Prove really half divine ;
The *Journal of Society of Arts*,
Justice of the Peace in parts ;
Examiner, sublime
In putting questions that we hate,
And sometimes losing line and bate.
When there is no small fry.
When little fish are let alone
They soon, of course, get overgrown—
Too artful, ay, to die.

What vital streams of glory flow !
But all who read of course must know
    The *Freeman, Friend,* the *Field*—
    Ha, ha, how many crops to yield !
But the *National Standard* takes his stand ;
Foremost we have at our command
The *Homeward Mail,* the news of old ;
But then *John Bull,* why should he scold ?
    The *Watchman* or the *People*—
    Most churches have a steeple ;
The *Racing Times* and *Public Ledger ;*
The *Magnet,* ah, to guide the beggar ;
    News of the World, to make one wise ;
    Whilst *Notes and Queries* oft surprise ;
The *Nonconformist, Union, Era,*
The *Indian News* and *Madras Times :*
    A host of others—what a heap !
    The *Weekly Dispatch* we find,
    Reynold's Newspaper so deep ;
But, oh ! the *Lancet ;* oh, the mind !
    Piercing to the very quick,
    Simply those that are so sick,
In morals so refined.

August 27th, 1865.

CURIOSITIES OF THE CABINET.

Hard woods, like men, but 'tis a saying
Soft woods are useless for inlaying ;
Whose working hand would dare disgrace
To cut and polish and give face
To rough or smooth things out of place ?
Despised, cut up ; ah ! fruitless toil,
Yet honour'd in their native soil.
What productions ! What a thought !
Blended beauty never bought.
Let me now show something new,
Come, my *foreign woods* to view.
African blackwood, dark as soot ;
    Beefwood or *Bully tree,*
Black ebony why substitute ?
    Ha, ha ! for *Lignum vitæ* see
Ironwood, for strength misuse ;
    Kingwood how resolute !
Lancewood, spars but to amuse ;
Letterwood, to infuse ;
    Or *Snakewood* to pollute ;
Sandalwood, but how demure !
Ha, ha, *Boxwood,* who can endure
The dying *Logwood* for mature ?
Nutmegwood, the taste insure ;
Walnutwood, to crack a joke ;
Zebrawood, whose striped cloak

With *Satinwood* th' ladies' pride ;
Russian Maple by her side.
Partridge and *Pheasantwood*,
Queenwood just for " turning," good
Tulipwood ; but *Yew-tree* bold ;
Jackwood, too, alas ! how cold ;
Logwood hard, but why omit ?
Should *Maple* (France) e'en now outwit
English Maple's perquisite ?
Sapanwood may tyrannise ;
Sabicu to sympathise ;
The *Churchyard yew* may be innate ;
Green ebony accelerate ;
Hickory (billets) how sedate !
Coromandel advocate ;
Canarywood significant—
No song without a visitant ;
Diversity, yet why acclaim ?
Maple (bird's eye), what a name !
Cedar (pencil) would proclaim ;
Softwood e'en in every state,
Foolish men predominate.
Braziletto, why applaud ?
Sapodillawood defraud ;
Such woods to cut or hack and shave,
Ha, ha ! all foreign woods outbrave.
Rosewood now may dedicate ;
Satinwood effeminate,
Only just to elevate
Th' *Rifle twigs* to educate,

For cutting up all foreign wood,
Whose " properties " esteemed as good.
Ha, ha ! not ev'ry giant could
Fell an *English tree* who would.

NIGHT THOUGHTS.

MIDNIGHT, when the cares of day are past,
How solemn, O, how beautiful, is that season !
As we gaze with throbbing hearts at the worlds above,
Those mysteriously beautiful mansions of Heaven,
Of inviolable God—eternal Light and Truth,
The overwhelming beauties of the cheering skies !
For a moment we forget our earthly sorrows ;
Deep in thoughtful prayer, we're lost in wonder,
As the sportive clouds mournfully pass away,
To remind us of death and new life hereafter ;
But like other things of this mysterious world,
This happy, happiest night-vision soon passes from us.
And we're left a little longer to breathe again
The morning prayer, in smiles of a glorious sun
Of unspeakable grandeur, which plainly speaks of God.
But how can we forget the beautiful stars of night,
Which fill us with so much hearty joy—surprised delight !
Beautiful stars, glorious stars, sublime glory !
We know but little of them, doubtless they shine for us.
Mysteriously fashioned by the hand of the living God.
O, how wonderfully they reflect the mighty light of Heaven,

Just to delight this inferior lower world,
Kindling in man that spiritual first-born light,
That living knowledge of the blessed God—
That ONE TRUE GOD—Comforter of love and mercy,
Who would that all should learn of Him and live !
    But every eye shall see Him ;
Yea, every one shall believe and bow down to Him :
Nor shall the spiritual eye be dimmed by time ;
Nay, it shall yet recognise in joy o'er the whole earth
That new provision of soothing light—the Gospel's
Spiritual seed of fathomless eternal beauty,
Which shall be scattered abroad by the power of God—
When darkness shall speed away as swiftly as time,
Spiritual power shall open the gates of Heaven,
And usher youth and age into the presence of God,
To live with Him for ever.

 July 23rd, 1861.

THE PAUPER'S ALTERNATIVE.

THEY are the best of friends who comfort bring,
 Cheering by help the poor, the suff'ring poor,
Of shrunken features, harass'd, wan, and dim,
 Who cannot work, nor beg from door to door.
Do not kind words with smiles oft prevail
To keep the starving suff'ring from the jail ?
Tho' true professional beggars find a joy—
But such we would not help, nor yet employ ;

It is the poor unfortunates of our race
That have no work, no money, friends, nor place :
No sympathy, and no one to advise—
Poor, alas ! yet honest—why despise
The man who, by misfortune, cannot gain
Respectability ?   Then why disdain
An honest pauper, who would do no wrong,
Only despised for being poor so long ?
Ye who have got much wealth, can ye not feel
For such a one to help him to a meal ?
Many a Lazarus lying at the gate,
But seldom seen until it is too late ;
For what's a pauper, if he's e'er so good ?
Minus of cash, he's seldom understood ;
Half starved to death, he's two things but to crave :
A parish coffin and a pauper's grave.

TO THE LITTLE " WILD DAISY " OF THE
CHURCHYARD.

FAIR and beautiful ;
Mysterious flower of animating hope ;
Why flourish to decline?   Ay, why, alas !
Touch'd by the finger of His creative hand,
To smile, expand in heav'nly living grace,
In adoration of thy Maker—God.
To glory in thy happy native light.
(Beauteous Daisy.)   Ah, in grace of Heaven,

To live and smile in joy unknown to man,
In cheering "language" of all-giving praise,
Of Nature's truth in holiness divine,
In godly pow'r to smile in life of death,
In harmonious enchanting glory
O'er the dead !

July 18th, 1865.

THE WARNING VOICE OF SPRING.

HARK ! the warning voice of spring,
    How pure and holy is her song !
Whilst rising stars and flowers now bring
    New hopes and joys, alas ! not long
To live ; how soon they pass away !
For earth-born glories soon decay.
But for a time they give delight,
To cheer the soul in her high flight
To blissful worlds of pure delight,
Where guiding stars of living light
Have life unfading truths above ;
The fadeless flowers and stars of love
Give holier praise with one accord
To Him their King, Creative Lord.

Hark, the warning voice of spring !
    Let all e'en now unite in song
Of holiness till night shall bring
That day when holier joys begin
    To smile on us—the time's not long.

Ah, death may come e'en in this hour,
To crown us with sustaining power !
To meet this Holy One above
In never-ending life of love.

THE FOOL'S FOLLY.

THE fool's delicious fancies reign
    In sinful empty show,
Where vice and folly smile to gain
    For him a hell below.

What cares he for the future bliss,
    If now he has his toy?
Ten thousand blessings he would miss
    For momentary joy.

Parade and pomp is his delight
    Upon a barren plain,
So sure is he of fancy light
    His glory to sustain.

Hoaxed and flattered, called " the *rose*,"
    Oh, fatal glory Fame !
No hostile knave would dare oppose
    A fool of such a name.

Such madd'ning rage, extreme delight,
    For " wisdom-gab " how jolly !
The offspring of a borrowed light
    Shows but a foolish folly.

Bound to filth, like some lame duck
   Waddling in the mire—
Oh, mortal stench ! oh, fearful sight !
   Such misery, frantic fire.

Like a thick vapour would he rise
   Far above the ground,
In fancied power beyond the skies ;
   Yet there he is not found.

Fixed in "mud-trap," moanful love,
   In fatal grief, he spies
The little stars around above,
   To which he ne'er can rise.

Oh ! take not from the natural fool
   His claret—nay, but give
Him highly-seasoned water-gruel,
   That he may really live.

THE CROWNING JOY OF MORROW.

As holiness comes with our birth,
   So, as we grow in light,
Friendship springs around in mirth.
   Whilst love smiles forth delight,
To recognise that holy worth
   In light of glowing love.
Man a living star to shine
In grace and truth and light divine,
   For heav'nly joy above ;

To live, alas! but soon to die,
　The soul soon takes her flight,
On the wings of love to fly,
　In life-eternal light;
Then to live and never die—
　Free from pain and sorrow—
What a glorious destiny
　The crowning joy of morrow!

———·———

WHO WOULD NOT TRUST IN HIM?

　　　　　IN pity
Christ bore the sins of many;
　On earth He came to give
His smiling help and saving grace;
　E'en died—that we should live.

He knows man's piteously weak,
　Quick'ning for the grave,
And so in love He comes to seek
　And gloriously to save
All men—ah! His blessed Son
Would His Father's will be done.

———·———

SUBLIMITIES OF DIVINE TRUTH.

LOOK on His works; can ye discern
　What holiness, delight?
Behold the flower, and live and learn
　The joy of glorious light.

Ha, there unseen, what insects toil,
   Ten thousand in a flower !
Oh, what a change the yielding soil,
   What truth divine and pow'r !
Look on the barleycorn, e'en there,
   Amongst the fragrant hay,
Myriads of unknown insects bear
   The golden fruit away.
Sublimities of truth divine
   In smiling joy appear ;
All is gloriously sublime,
   Heavenly and sincere.

THE EARLY CALLED.

THE early call'd, how like the flower
To live, alas ! but for an hour,
Then pass away in godly power.
The infant bud of yesterday
   In fading gloom is seen
To-day, but when the night shall come
   To vanish from the scene.
To-morrow we may look around,
   The weeping eye is cast
To seek for what cannot be found
   Until we too have past
Into that new existence, ay,
In glory of eternal day.

Deprived, bereft of sacred love,
    On earth in sickening sorrow,
But soon affection seeks above
    To find again to-morrow
The loved ones, yea, for it is said
    By holy faith that's given,
Altho' they die, they are not dead,
    But live for joy in Heaven.
Jesus calls the little ones ;
    He bids us all be free
As children blest to live above
    In life eternity.

"WHY WILL YE DIE ?"

Go to the churchyard, free from fear or dread,
And learn a lesson from the silent dead ;
Such glorious teaching, ere it be too late,
May give us light to venerate the bed
Of earthly flowers quick'ning into life
Of immortality.

    Here rich and poor as one ; oh, contemplate !
Regard all men as equal—small and great—
Vain pompous man : what living dust of earth !
Where will he find that peace and rest ?—beware !
The " dress'd up " body, the crown'd heads of birth
Can find no joy without His living care.

Arise, arise, in power of light to live,
And learn to be as one all-breathing love ;
The "ignorant" teach ; to the "poor" freely give ;
We're children of one Father, God above.
Where is the man who would not live for Heaven,
Or seek that God who bids him come on high,
In glorified grace of wisdom given,
To live for ever? Oh, that tear and sigh !
Alas, alas ! says God, " Why will ye die ?"

ON THE DEATH OF MRS. WHITE ST. STEPHENS.

SHE lived not for herself,
And look'd for no return for secret help ;
But ah ! a sure reward for her good works
Was e'en known to her in that last hour,
When sympathising friends would give their all
To make her day on earth a moment longer.
The poor may weep, but oh !
In their bereavement angel-saints rejoice
To see her crowned, transformed, a star of light
To shine for ever in eternal glory.
May, 1868.

OCTOBER.

DARK and dreary October,
How gloomy thy day of long-cast shadows,
Vanishing into darkness : yea, alas !
Soon the evening darkens into night ;

To give that sweet balm of happy sleep,
In silent joy of autumn ;
The drooping flow'rs, smiling in decline,
Charmed by the heavenly hope of Nature—
By the gentle kisses of the dewdrop,
As they pass away to unseen glory
Of new creation.   In this darksome hour
Silence reigns around in holy order,
Whilst the moments fly to give return
Of life and freshness to the glowing morn
Of spring.   Then the beauteous rising sun
Of eternal glory and of welcome joy
Shall shine for ever ; yea, for ever,
When the kindred souls shall meet again,
In celestial glory, to part no more.
Merciful Providence, wonderful are Thy ways !
Soon we die ; ah ! like a moment sleep :
Happy is that thought ! O, happy thought,
Awakened by the holy kiss of angels,
To be ushered in the presence of our God,
On that glorious day so near at hand,
When ev'ry flower shall unfold its beauty,
And yield its holy fragrance to its Giver,
Who calls forth living light and holy beauty
From mortal clay to bloom and smile again
In Paradise ! O, happy, happy thought,
Where angels and saints shall ever sing
The song of everlasting joy and praise
In glory of His gifts!

" TITTLE-TATTLE."

THE dreaded
Scandal-maker's tittle-tattle strife
     In love or friendship show pretence for good :
Under his cloak the secret, hidden knife
     To stab, but in the dark to draw your blood.

The first to wound, the first to come and heal :
     Thus, by deceit so plausible and fair,
He calls down vengeance loudly ; but of such zeal,
     Mockery and hypocrisy, beware !

The fiend escapes Jack Ketch ten thousand times,
     So often as the serpent's fed, 'tis said :
Such killing is no murder for such crimes ;
     We'd trample the assassin until dead.

Religion, unresenting, forbids the war ;
     Commands that the art of murder none shall know :
Return for evil love, such blessing, for
     You heap e'en coals of fire upon the foe.

THE STAR OF THE EAST.

HAIL, holy Star of liberty Divine,
     Thy beaming light fills the glorious sky !
How full of cheering gentle smiling grace,
     Incessant love, and holy watchful eye.
     To set man free !

O Star, Star of the East,
How full of glory-giving calm repose,
And living light, quickening ev'ry soul
To beauteous life of immortality !
The opening graves will soon give up their dead,
Who from a joyous sleep awake in peace,
To receive the choicest blessings from His hand,
When time, alas ! shall be no more.
Oh, mortal man, look up in pray'r, look up !
Behold the Star of purifying love,
Freeing the soul from ev'ry sorrowing care,
That man may live in Jesus Christ the Lord,
Chang'd to be unchanged for evermore,
In blissful light of immortality.

"THE LORD HAS RISEN."

FROM the grave
The Lord has risen ! come and see :
    Behold Him now in faith and love,
Convincing truth's reality.

    Now on the throne of joy above,
His fainting soul refreshed, His face
All smiling love and living grace
    In life eternity.

Ne'er again to disappear,
    His eye is on us all ;
Look up ! behold the Saviour dear !
    And listen to His call.

Bless'd Redeemer, Star of Light,
　In glory e'er to shine ;
To 'lumine life, and give delight,
　New joys of life divine.

He suffer'd death, to wipe the stain
　Of sin, to make us free :
Oh, shall we, then, our love constrain
From Him who calls each by his name
To Heav'n, from worldly guilt and shame ?
In life of holiness remain,
　To all eternity.

THE GLORY OF GOD IN NATURE.

It is just now a pleasing sight to see
　Th' admiring beauties of the wood,
The flow'ry plant and budding tree,
　Each thriving in the light of good,
　His will by nature understood.
On hill and dale, throughout the land,
　Small weeds and herbs spring into light,
And bless'd by His creative hand,
　To smile in glory of delight—
　Ay, what a joyous living sight !
The seasons, months, the days, and hours,
　Are all adapted, as they speed,
To teach, by Nature's new-born flowers,
　A holy lesson.　'Tis men's creed
To live and learn—He giveth powers

Of understanding as they read
His Grace Divine e'en in the weed,
    And ev'ry weed-like flower indeed.
The common moss, the smallest blade
Of grass, in wisdom all were made
To show His heavenly power on earth,
And wisdom-joy of smiling birth.
The early flowers of March behold,
Full of living powers untold :
Toil they not, nor do they spin,
Though th' unhallow'd hand of sin
May pluck, contaminate, the flower
Created by His wondrous power.
What glory, yea, what mystery deep
Awaken'd out of winter sleep :
Beauteous violets smile to peep
(The new creations of the earth),
To warn us of their second birth.
Such harmony, in truth, to move
Nature's glorious pow'rs above,
Holy flowers in smiles unite
In giving praises of delight.
Would that men looked up with joy,
And breathed their prayers of faith on high,
To see their God before they die !
To close their eyes for peaceful rest
With saints in glory to be blest.

CALL TO SPRING.

THOU joyous Spring of song and beauty,
   Time smiles to give thee birth,
Whilst Nature's calling thee to duty,
   Of living light and mirth.
In truth of glory she beholds
   Thy life-advancing powers.
Why linger, ay?—come, come, unfold
   Thy new-born holy flowers ;
Time and Nature's loving smile
   Will welcome thee in youth,
And watch thy birth and life awhile
   In harmonizing truth ;
The crowning season of the year,
   Of grandeur and delight ;
What gladness, ay !—ah, thou'rt near,
   Enraptured joyous light
Of holy blessings ; yea, thy powers
In adorative song of flowers,
   O, glorious heavenly sight !
Then pass on, Time, thy few short hours,
   That hill and dale and shady bowers
May soon be decked with fair spring flowers
   In grace of sunlight beauty :
That light of truth which Nature gives
To gladden man just while he lives,
   And teach him holy duty,
In gratitude for all that's given,
Whilst looking on the truths of Heaven.

THE EARLY FLOWERS OF SPRING.

WHAT language can express our love,
In holy song to Him above,
Whilst contemplating Nature's powers,
Her heavenly shining starlike flowers!—
   The flowers of early Spring,
Ev'rywhere now springing up
   To smile in godly light :
The primrose and buttercup
   Forth peeping to delight,
   And charmingly invite
Attention to His vast design,
And His creative skill divine—
Flowers of beauty, how sublime,
   Kissed by th' evening dew !
   The snowdrop, crocus, violet blue,
Why come they forth in light,
To raise the appetite ?
   The eye to feed on what is new,
   What sacred beauties come to view,
In holiness delight !

Yet, oh, alas ! how soon they're gone !
   But why such warnings given ?—
That we should watch the coming morn.
For life, how short, why were we born ? —
   To learn to live for Heaven ;
   By Nature's teaching to improve
   The mind and soul to perfect love.

NOVEMBER.

Dark November,
Unpitying month, dost thou just come
To strip the beauteous trees of their foliage ?
How soon the flowery beauties vanish
In thy stern chilling hour of sad delight !
Why should they die to be renewed in life,
To bud and bloom again in Nature's strength
In the opening morn of happy spring ?
O matchless proof of holy truth divine !
'Tis even so with man : tho' he be
Surrounded by some thick gathering clouds
Of ev'ry sorrowing care of winter darkness,
Soon they'll vanish in the glorious light
Of infinite joy of sweet summer day.
The wise arrangement of ev'ry season
Speaks the wisdom of Almighty Power :
Yea, ev'ry holy, glorious beauty,
Touched by the vital spirit of Heaven,
Unfolds or closes its smiling treasure
At His will.   Ah, Creation's discipline,
Infinite pow'r of organization,
Proclaims the glorifying praise of Him
Who made all things for sinful mortal man,
Mysteriously beautiful, indeed.

THE SOLDIER'S DEATH IS WARLIKE GLORY.

Oh ! that sick'ning thought—ah ! chilling lament ;
Tumult of terror—a tyrant's fury ;
The angry storm of agonizing war ;
In the various forms of killing art,
In the smoking midst of labouring Death,
The soldier's precious life of bloody strife
Consists in ev'ry frightful shape of horror ;
Self-cheating admiration's fiery cause—
Brother murdering brother for applause :
The one survives in scatter'd heap oppress'd,
The other in his agonizing dust—
The dying, shrieking cries of warlike glory,
In strength and beauty doom'd but for the grave :
Contending brothers on the field of Death
Dispute not grief-controlling pow'r.
What is life to him whose death is glory ?
He bids defiance in his country's cause ;
No hidden dread he finds in his reward :
His trembling lips utter a glorious pray'r—
"God save my Queen and country !" he resumes,
In smiles of love, " the deed is not my own."
And thus the noble hero dies in peace,
Serving his Queen and country and his God,
To gain his freedom in another world.
Yet the fond mother in her lonely grief,
Behold her drooping head as now she cries,
In madd'ning smiles of insensibility,
" Restore to me, O God, my only son,

For in Thy name I justly claim my own."
With fervent grasp, but disappointing sorrow,
Her feelings overcome her waking dream ;
The absence of her darling, loving child—
How can she understand the living dead ?
That fond transport of joy—that earnest gaze—
That ardent tone which makes the bosom swell !
With panting breath she takes a wild strange glance
At all around—then cries, " Where is my son ?"
And then with sweeter smiles of Fancy's pow'r
She once again beholds her angel child;
In pray'r she meekly thanks her God once more.
That secret charm of holy gratitude
Is only known to the all-pitying God,
Whose gentle mercy is all-smiling love.

DEATH ; OR, THE LOST FLOWER.

DEATH comes—ah, yes, alas ! tis so,
    And the soul must take her flight
Down into the world of bitter woe,
    Or in the realms of living light,
Where holy saints and angels dwell
    In glorious heavenly love
With God their King Immanuel
    In joyous power above.

Death comes to all—a few short years
   And we are gone : no trace
Is left : but memory in sweet tears
   In loving light gives chase,
Beholds the loved one far away,
   And seeks in life for power,
In hope to meet in that last day
   The long lost heavenly flower.

THE OLD YEAR.

ADIEU, Old Year! thy feeble life is o'er,
   In silent power of death thou'st pass'd away.
Time and Nature bade the awakening year
   To smile a blessing on thy parting day.
Take now thy rest and sleep in peace secure,
   In tranquil joyous blessing and delight ;
At thy departure Time could do no more
   Than welcome in another year of light.
Thy days are spent, alas ! and thou art gone,
   New powers of light are smiling now on high
To give to man new glories yet unborn,
   For mundane joys soon with him must die.
And yet, Old Year, to memory thou shalt bring
   Thy endless treasures which have pass'd away,
The bounteous harvest—thy glowing spring
   Shall joy in the prospects of a future day.

But man looks on in heartfelt prayer and love
  'Till, lost in thought about His works so great,
He seems to hear the Holy One above
  Say, "Watch, make ready for thy future state."

January 1st, 1866.

ETHEREAL LESSONS.

THE moon's majestic silver beams
  Of glorious smiling power,
That melting, tender kiss of joy
  To charm to sleep the flower;
The glorious sun of morning light
  Majestically unfolds
The awak'ning beauty of delight
  Which Nature's God controls:
The sun and moon divinely given,
  The stars beyond the sky,
And ev'ry flower that blooms on earth
  Is blest by God on high.
They tell us of more glorious things—
Of God their Maker, King of kings,
  To whom all glory's given;
They teach us how to live and pray
In harmony of night and day,
  In the watchful light of Heaven.

A DREAM.

ENRAPTUR'D in a dream of love,
Which carried me to life above,
I felt myself as counted dead :
On the Throne of Grace I saw
The Lamb of God, alas !
And as I bow'd in solemn awe,
To let the angels pass,
I heard a holy song : its sound
Fill'd me with delight :
I raised my head to look around,
And oh, good God ! the sight.
I felt unworthy and alone ;
From angels robed in white,
I turned to look upon the throne—
Fell blinded with the light !
Cast down, I pray'd and wept aloud
In sorrow and distress ;
All was dark—a darken'd cloud—
Ha, words can ne'er express !
But whilst in sorrow there above
I sought and found but One,
Who smiled in pity and in love :
'Twas Jesus Christ, His Son.
" Arise !" said He, " awake and pray ;
The Holy One inspire ;
To-morrow is the Judgment Day ;
Ask what thou may'st require."

I turned in penitence to ask,
    And saw upon His brow
His smiling love ; but oh, the task !
    Can I describe it now ?
Ah, no ! I cannot write nor trace,
    Th' enchanted vision's gone,
And yet I see His holy face
    Like innocence new-born.
Unworthy, oh, to live or die,
    I felt that sad mistrust ;
My guilty conscience made me sigh—
    Alas ! proud lofty dust.
Why didst Thou me create—oh why ?
    To deplore my guilty state—
With such a load ! and when I die
    How can I pass the gate ?
That heav'nly gate of holy light,
    My fainting soul, how weak !
O God, my Father, teach me right,
    Now only Thee I seek.

LULLABY.

Smiling infant,
    God is near
But to bless thee :
    Dost thou fear ?

Canst thou see Him,
    Full of love,
Looking on thee
    From above ?

Hush to silence,
　Sleep and rest ;
Awake again
　To be blest.
Jesus ! Father !
　God of love !
Smiles His mercy
　From above ;
For thy mother's
　Prayer is given
Oft to ask
　A smile from Heaven.
Dost thou know
　A mother's love ?
And thy Father's
　Care above
For thee, little
　Angel dear ?
Jesus looks
　On thee : why fear ?
Holy angels
　Guard thy bed :
See His glory
　'Round thy head.
Yet for thee
　I daily pray
That His light
　May crown thy day :
Holy peace
　Be on thy brow.

Listen to
　My prayer now :—
" May He bless
　Thee, little one ;
Give thee grace
　To overcome
Evil passions
　Such as we
Poor frail mortals
　Cannot see."
Soon His loving
　Call thou'lt hear ;
Listen, watch for
　Him—why fear ?
Such as thou
　He bids to come
To His arms—
　Yea, every one.
Hope and pray
　That He will save,
Give thee life
　Beyond the grave.
Soon thou'lt close
　Thine eyes in death—
Sweet repose
　Of living breath—
To awake
　In Heavenly light,
And to live
　In His delight

In that world   Smiling infant,
  So far above,   God is near,
Joyously,   For He loves thee,
  In holy love !   Baby dear !

NATURE'S BEAUTY.

          Who giveth life ?
Why spreads the glory of the blooming trees,
The elm, the sycamore, and stately oak,
The glorious poplar, willow, and the hazel,
Smiling forth their graceful living bloom
Of diversified beauty?   Mark well
The tiny shooting buds on ev'ry branch,
Expanding and exulting in the light
Of holy order.   Here the insects play
And work in wisdom, sheltered by the foliage,
The thickset foliage, collecting honey, wine,
Their harvest food, in life of giving praise
In language that creates the admiration
Of e'en man, who lives to learn of Nature's
Transporting joy of His divine creation.

What life of joy in liberty and power,
Amazing sights of life, all giving beauty,
Smiling in their birth, to live and die !
Glorious are the peculiar gifts of God's
Endless power of life, transforming glory,
Boundless treasures of eternal wisdom.

Insensible is man, and without reverence ;
No gratitude ; and yet in power and truth
He beholds the mighty agency of God,
His holy providence, His will and love,
Great care divine for everything He's made
To glorify the earth for man's own sake,
To teach him how to live and see aright
The way to Heaven, before it is too late
To know his God, the all-wise loving Maker,
The Giver of eternal life to come.

SENSIBILITY.

" Ah ! spare yon emmet, rich in hoarded grain ;
He lives with pleasure and he dies with pain."
In strictest search for food his time to spend,
What mortal mind would not defend
These little creatures, disciplined to raise
In admiration of their Maker's praise?
They are His works, creative power of light,
Toiling on in joy from morn till night,
Unheeded here by man, yet they can give—
Would he but learn—the lesson how to live.
But are they sent, the life of His creation,
To be destroyed by those who seek salvation ?
Ah no, alas ! the same good God of light
Would have them live to praise in joy, delight
Their Maker, God of spirit, truth, and love.

Will man not let them live in perfect peace,
To work in joy till nature's life shall cease?
Let man reflect, he has a soul to save,
To live in glorious realms beyond the grave.

January 5th, 1865.

"THE MAN WHO IS BEST UNDERSTOOD."

THE man whose heart feels for another
  Is wise and most nobly good—
Who liveth to care for a brother
  Is the man who is best understood.
No matter how lowly in state
  Whilst he lives for another in love,
He alone can be virtuously great
  In the sight of his Maker above.
His reward is not men's mean applause ;
  In secret he extends his kind hand
To assist in his right glorious cause
  At heart, tho' but little at command.
He is richer and greater we know
  Than princes who selfish can be,
For the light of his virtue will show
  He's a king, and his kingdom is free :
Whilst he lives, secret blessing is given ;
When he dies, holy peace, joy, and Heaven.

LOOK UP.

"Look up."

Ha, whilst I gaze upon the stars above,'
My mind is filled with joy-like fear, devotion :
Oh, how I tremble whilst I think of God !
The soul so full of solemn deep emotion.
Round above me, yea, on every side,
Mine eyes will wander with my thoughts to find
That Holy One, so tenderly, so kind,
Till lost in joy. But faith, in light of love,
Would have me leave this world and all her gifts
To go and dwell with holy friends above ;
With friends, I say, where all is blissful peace,
Where sorrow and unkindness are not known.
Good holy God, search in my heart to prove
That strange, but joyous feeling, hope in love.

July 11th, 1865.

AN INSECT RAID.

A SPIDER with an envious eye
    Springs forward with a bound
Upon a little harmless fly,
        To suck its blood
        Of slimy mud,
    And then would scamper round
Into its web of safe retreat,
To dwell upon its fatal beat—

To die of poison slow.
How could this poor thing know,
Not having any sense or reason,
That flies just now are out of season ?
Tho' one comes forth revenged to be ;
For what's my life, the fly thought he,
   If I a spider kill?
   Ha, by my cultur'd skill,
It is a glory and a pride
That reason should my merits guide,
   'Tho' perhaps against my will.
But few there are that can believe,
For is it nature to deceive
   A spider ?   Yes, of course,
      Its living prey
      No other way
   Can take life without force.
So for the fly the spider dies,
   Their lives of " power " have lost ;
Ne'er again can each one rise,
   For paying double cost.

THE PRIMROSE AND VIOLET.

BEAUTEOUS primrose !   Thy power deceives
The unthinking, who have deem'd thee long past dead ;
Thy cheering buds peep out between the leaves,
And smile to find the summer flowers have fled.

Beauteous violets, flowers of earliest day !
Why come ye forth, ay, out of lifeless clay ?
To cheer the heart of Nature's giving task,
In hope to find that winter glory's past.

Beauteous snowdrop of transporting light !
In life and beauty, oh, what joy, delight !
Ye Heaven-born flowers, why awake from sleep ?
To cheer the eye, make glad the heart of truth ;
Bereft, alas ! e'en in thy crowning youth
Of mystery deep ; how soon, alas, to die !
March on, ye winter months, in power on high,
To bring fair spring, new glories to supply—
Ah, flowers, bright flowers, to gladden all the earth !
Behold the birds just seeking power in birth ;
Yea, look around ; this happy time of year
Speaks sudden joy, that spring will soon be here !
" February snow " will soon be gone, and bright
Glorious March will soon smile forth new light—
Ten thousand blossoms glorying in delight.
What life of beauty hidden 'neath the sod
Spring up to glorify Creative God !

THE DEEDS OF DARKNESS.

THE anniversary of the blackest day
Will soon be o'er ; but its horrid stench
Of o'erloaded sorrow must be left
Behind as privilege to pay the cost

K

Of its remembrance.   For oh, alas !
The horror-stricken, hoof-inflicting pain
Brings the longitudinal furrows deep
In the cheek, whilst the soul is filled
With ev'ry vice of killing scars and sores
Too numerous to depict or sketch aright.
Oh ! watch the cruel power of sov'reign law ;
Why shudder at the devil and his imps ?
Clinging zeal improves hideous noise.
'Midst smoke and slush, how the victims fall !—
Character gone—ah ! to rise no more.
Watch the fierce sway of savage swiftness,
The saraband of frantic inspiration.
Hark ! the braying sentiment of fright
In the lustful strain of admiration,
The amicable order of peculiar darkness
In the blackest form of living sorrow.
The reckless, headstrong mountebank is up
To amuse poor Jack, and make him cunning wise ;
He resigns his fate in patient meekness
To pointed manners of an ignorant knave,
Whose polished " jewel " roguishly reflects
The two-faced view of a market cheat,
Whilst unobserved pickpockets in the crowd
Rob the policeman of their trying skill.
As all are " gentlemen " but the suff'ring few,
The royal blood of royal staff and power
Are full of nerve ; but then they have no faith
In nothing but a glass of ale or stout,
Which does wonders when the curtain's down,

Gilding wrongs of every well-known clown.
The language of the eye is in the wink—
A few halfpence will sell a sleepy drone,
Who demands his " beer and bacca " as a rule ;
But then who would avoid the playing trick,
Or be offended at the cause of right ?

A LESSON OF WAR.

LIST, my friends, to what I state,
   A lesson ye may learn ;
Modify, before too late,
   Ev'ry passion in its turn
Which tends to envy-hate.

      At noon,
On the twenty-first of June,
   The longest day, remember,
Two hungry flies, in contest great,
Fell upon my dinner-plate ;
Fighting sharp entwined each other,
The one was quite as good as t'other :
Presently they both gave in,
   With broken legs and wings misplaced.
As neither had the power to win
The fight, they deem'd retreat no sin,
   Nor warlike cowardice disgrace.

K 2

Disabled, almost out of breath,
  A spider comes to reason,
Giving them relief in death,
  In harmony of season.
Then list, ye friends, to what I state,
  In anger's rage cool down ;
Live to learn and contemplate
This warlike age of insect hate,
  In ev'ry clime and town.
But now, behold the empty plate !
Ah ! right and might are oft too late,
When little guise decides the fate :
As these two silly flies were shown,
Their simple battle's not their own.

SLEEP.

Awake again to morning light,
  Breathe again your prayer to God,
For the happy sleep of night;
  For that vision's bright abode ;
Wisdom's dream of light and joy,
Heavenly bliss without alloy.

Holy children, when ye die,
  Conscience seems to tell me this--
God will take ye up on high ;
  For such as ye the angels kiss.
O Heaven grant ye every joy.
Perfect bliss without alloy !

Little children's home is Heaven ;
   Christ hath given that assurance ;
Came He not on earth, and even
   Suffered pain, ah ! Death's endurance,
That man, too, may hope for joy,
   Perfect bliss without alloy ?

April, 1861.

SATIRE.

" POETS, like weavers, should with taste and reason
Adapt their various goods to every season."
The taste for " game " is only for a day,
But then the sickly weak should have fair play :
A cunning ruse may give a loss to trade,
And spoil the gravy of the dish that's made.
Set not too high a price upon your wares,
First separate your wheat from growing tares ;
Remember, too, that evil fraud's a bait,
And its allurement brings a double hate :
Pay nice attention to the fool or knave,
And what he loses you collect and save :
Rap not too hard the knuckles of thy foe,
He may retaliate with double blow ;
Besides, there is no gain in mortal strife,
The tyrant wounds himself by taking life.
Ha, pity him, alas ! who would give pain,
By satire relish of surviving shame.

The *lion* and the *ape* may thus dispute,
But then the roar and chatter may confute
The other hungry beasts, such as the bear,
Which in their living prey they all should share.

———•———

" THOU SHALT NOT KILL."

WHY take the life thou canst ne'er give ?
Why should the smallest thing not live ?
Unoffending insects have a right
To life's enjoyment in His holy light
Of heav'nly power, yea, and smiling love—
By Him they were created and approved.

The unoffending worm, the ant, and bee—
Mark their instincts ; with nice discernment see
Their glorious merriment and wisdom-skill,
Designed for some great object to fulfil :
In His great glory they proclaim His will.
Has man no cherish'd hope ?   Then why offend
These little creatures, which on Him depend ?
Beware ! alas, they have a God of love,
Who made them, and is watching from above.

" Thou shalt not kill," said God.   Who will deny
The meanest insect life He would supply,
To teach man how to live and how to die?

TO NANCY—THE CANTERBURY BELLE.

DEAR Nancy, I fancy
As this bonnet's not blue,
Its cherries and berries
Will smile green upon you ;
Its matchless pea-blossom—a beautiful hue—
Will conceal, yet reveal
The best part of your dress !
What a cheat of deceit !—
And yet, nevertheless,
Such a " duck " of a bonnet's a decided success !
'Tis a cure, to be sure.
Ha ! but then there's no " pride "
Without cost ! The head's lost
With a " curtain " so wide.
What a swell, Nancy belle !
'Mongst magpies and apes,
Why clatter and chatter
Whilst you " measure " your " tapes ?"
I'd fit you more " block-heads," had I got the shapes.
Dear Nancy, I fancy
To be " dacently " clad,
On your part there's an art
Of becoming so mad :
Your taste, skill and judgment—oh that it I had !
How sublime was the " chime !"
Such a " caw " has no power
From the church of St. George or from Bell Harry's
'Tis an art to impart :   [Tower !

But the cobbler will soon
    Take a rise, to surprise
The poor man in the moon,
Whose metal pinchbeck will be melted this June.
        Such a name for high fame
        Has a classical right ;
        Such doctors and proctors
        Compose " in the light,"
Tho', ten chances to one that they learn how to write !
        But, Nancy, I fancy
        We shan't disagree ;
        Your passion for fashion
        Is a credit on thee—
When you want a new bonnet, pray think of C. C.

BEES.

A FABLE.

            An ambitious,
Impious queen " put forth " new laws,
    To kill all drones, and civilise
The working bees that plead the cause
    Of equalising in the prize ;
Tumultuous bees throughout the land
    Began to war with one another ;
Awaken'd drones, in wild command,
    Fought desperately to kill each other.

These senseless insects " figured" well
　To thus "outdo" each other's will ;
Each strove in power to excel,
　And suffer'd death to show his skill :
The wounded, too, found no redress,
　They fought but to obey the great ;
Rather than live in idleness
　They'd crown in death their common fate.
Amazed the " workers " idly stand,
　Sick'ning at the sight of pain ;
The poor warriors of the land
　Should bury more than had been slain.
The queen, confused, knew not her own,
　Yet bade the working bees appear
Around to guard her honoured throne ;
　But only wounded drones came near,
　For all the " workers " died in fear,
And left the queen in sad disgrace,
To typify the human race.
The lawless drones revived to brave
And make their guilty queen a slave,
Tho' now their ruling queen lies dead—
Was murdered for the blood she shed.
But such is life one lives to gain,
By slaughter in his turn is slain :
Some glory in such warlike fame,
Seeking power to gain a name.
But e'en the greatest on the throne
Have nothing here to call their own,

Whilst charity in common sense
Is but a foolish recompence
For those who die, alas ! to yield
Their fortunes of the battle-field.

January 15th, 1866.

AMONG THE SNOW.

Upon the leads
We see the heads
Of men with spade and shovel,
Hard working so
To clear the snow
From the roof of every hovel.
Out in the streets
Each workman greets
The labouring men who clear
Away the snow—
Why there they go,
See how they persevere,
Each one an engineer !
In winter cold severe.
To clear the road
Load after load
They cart on to the river ;
Whilst idle men
Look on, but then
They stand about to shiver.

The few, but wise,
Of ev'ry size.
Whose noble deeds inspire.
Mount on the top
Of church to stop
The snow from building higher.
In glory high;
But by-the-by,
They look down on the people :
Who've no desire
To rise e'en higher
To ornament the steeple.
At Blean, the poor
Have no front door :—
A hundred miles away;
No light, nor coals,
But snow-flake folds
To warm them night and day.

January 16th, 1867.

THE INDUSTRIOUS LITTLE BEE.

Happy, chaste, innocent little labourer,
Who taught thee to so wisely snatch from the beautiful
Blooming shrubs and every tiny flower and flowery weed
Such fruit as shall serve thee for thy winter-food?
Who taught thee to find such wealth,
So as to leave unhurt the most delicate tender flowers.

Which smilingly invite thee to take—not as a thief in the night,
But openly in the morning's glorious light—
That which is so wisely designed and ordained for thee?
And who giveth thee life, and that wonderful forethought
Of providing thyself and young with proper food for the morrow?
We answer, The great God, who made thee for that purpose.
But who disputes thy hard-earned, honest-gotten gain?
Pronounces it pelf?—thee a robber?—a covetous creature?
And cruelly takes thy life for the product
Of this thy summer's happy toil?—ah! winter's store?
We answer, Man, never satisfied with his own day's labour.
Happy, happy, chaste, industrious little Bee, toil on!
For thy every passion is that of love and beauty;
Such heavenly virtue and endearing grace as thine
Divinely glows to enchant Nature's heart.   [thee
Yes, toil on! whilst the beauteous flowers are smilingly inviting
To take the fill of such rich sweets as will repay thy labour.
Tho' death be thy reward, yet, alas! thou canst not exist without it.
Toil on! lay up thy little gain, e'en for the selfish, greedy drone.
Or man will surely find fault with thee for idleness,
And the pretext for taking thy innocent life.

  April 22nd, 1861.

----•----

FLORAL DESTINY.

    'Tis the fate of all flowers to die—
        Yea, for conquering Death tells us all,
    In the power and glory of time,
        The most stately and mighty must fall.

'Tis the fate of all flowers to die,
   Tho' in virtue and light they may glow ;
But the power that bids is Divine—
   Cannot grant them a long life below.

'Tis the fate of all men once to die—
   Yea, the glorious good must resign
His breath—oh ! that spirit-living breath
   Of glorious quickening time—
Ha ! to smile forth beauty in Death,
   A flower eternal, divine.

May 19th, 1863.

CHILDHOOD.

LITTLE star.　We watch the smiling infant,—
The tender offspring of a mother's love,
The beauteous flower of early spring,—
And dwell upon the past with some regret ;
Yet thanking God that we are still alive
To learn of Him and make our way to Heaven—
Improving thus the little time that's given,
Even as a child of living hope.
   How sweet the mem'ry of our early days !
How bright the view, the pleasure, hope of joy,
Stealing o'er the mind in cheerful dreams
Of perpetual youth and beauty !
   The smiling infant of unearthly care—
The Heavens seem to burst upon its view—
The heart so full of peaceful glowing light.

And holy joy flowing in the soul,
To glorify its never-ending day
Of grace and rest.   Thou good Supreme !
   God is love : His holy Spirit comes
To quicken ev'ry cheering beam of hope,
To penetrate the summer-bud of life,
To perfect and to glorify the flower.
O ! mark the smiles—the smiling light of God—
The angel kiss : the whisper and the touch
Give thrilling joy in that unbroken pow'r
Of love which smiles eternally above.
The future life of bliss : that holy joy—
That glorifying, harmonising praise
To Him above, great God and Lord of all.
April 6th, 1863.

THE GLORY OF GOD IN NATURE.

     How beautiful the flower—
The bursting bud !   Ah ! Nature's solemn power,
Giving modest beauty, strength, and liberty,
To run its holy course in blissful song,
Without a murmur, fearless of its age,
Smiling for its future gracefully,
To vanish in decline when night shall come,
And give that holy wealth of sleep and rest.
Ah ! who can but admire the works of God !
That quick'ning grace in glory ! O how sweet
The morning beam of spotless pure delight,

That gives the beauteous bloom a touch of joy—
O light of Heaven, O living light of joy,
Shine forth thy glorious living beauty,
That man may lift his heart in prayer !

MAY SHOWERS.

Bless'd May's sweet, gentle, cooling showers,
    Rain-drops—life-kissing light
Diffusing joy to new-born flowers,
Emitting fragrance day and night,
    Now smiling in delight
To cheer the soul—what treasure given !
The balmy-breathing love of Heaven.

May 13th, 1864.

TRUTH.

Honest independent Truth
    Never wanders from the light,
For she smiles eternal youth,
    In the wisdom of delight.
Yes, her joyous powers given
    Lift the soul above all pride,
E'en on the throne of heaven,
    Where the saints of God preside.

March 7th, 1868.

ADVENT.

SLEEP, forsake us : let us watch
In the power of faith that's given,
Whilst the Holy One above us
Bids us now look up to Heaven.

Awake, awake, my soul, awake !
Behold the " rising Star " above !
Ah, my soul ! awake, arise !
To welcome light of joyous love.

December 5th, 1865.

THE DEAN OF CANTERBURY.

LONG live the Dean
To grace that highest calling here on earth,
And teach the truth of His inspired Word ;
So step by step to lead us on to God,
In holiness of living light and love,
To future glory.   .
God grant the wish
That he and all his helping friends may live
To do His will, to glorify the church,
Of never-ending joy.

September 7th, 1870.

THE SENSELESS BRUTE.

HIDEOUS monster (not unlike an ape),
  Whose violent passion is to "bite" and scratch,
Just as the fit may take the action's shape,
For self-rewarding toil to bow and scrape,
  Or foam with rage, poor, disappointed wretch,
But to await the madhouse or the jail ;
To gain that point such natures seldom fail.

September, 1870.

CONSOLATION IN PERSECUTION.

HAST thou the mind
  To suffer for His sake alone?
Hard press'd, hedg'd in by foes around,
  Have faith to prove His love?
'Then drink thy portion from the cup ;
  Depart to Him above,
    Who'll smile new blessings to atone
    What joys to find.

September 7th, 1870.

L.

THE RIGHT REVEREND THE BISHOP OF DOVER.

THANK God for such a friend,
Who strives to do His holy will and teach
The Christian truths of charity and love.
   Long may he live, bless'd, endeared by all
In th' approving smiles of his all-wise Creator,
To glorify His living church.
Proclaim the gospel, in the light of Heaven
To make us one in Him who is all love,
In mercy smiles would lift us from the earth
To perpetual joy and never-ending glory
Of power Divine.

September 18th, 1870.

GLORIOUS HUMBUG.

         FROM folly's store
The humbug gives his empty " talk,"
   To do "great things" just to amuse
And disappoint.
         But then we " chalk
It up," whene'er he pays respect
To those who wisely would object
      To give the fellow all his dues
         For something worse than creaking shoes :
For when, alas ! his " grinders " clack
He's sure to make a perfect wreck
      And give us all the blues.

September 9th, 1870.

"DOG EAT DOG."

PRIMARY OBJECT.

COOLLY contesting
In starveling anger for the Rhine ;
But warmer feelings one may own
Must now exist, because the *prime*
Was after all found in the *Bone*.

September 9th, 1870.

STARS.

THE GLORIOUS STARS ABOVE.

IN light of holiness
Now contemplate the wondrous stars above ;
How beautiful, so heavenly and divine !
How full of glory, smiling as they shine,
To awaken man to adorative love !

THE INGLORIOUS STARS BELOW.

Bright stars of glory, wisdom, light, and grace,
But what is man upon a barren land ?
No faith nor hope to see His holy face,
Careless about the higher things, to trace
The wondrous workings of the Almighty hand :
His simple pleasure is this world's command.

L 2

Poor ignorant mortals, little can they know
   Of God : to Him ungrateful for their lives ;
Affections here misplaced ; ha ! many a foe,
   Or worldly star, each with his many wives
   Must fall still lower, but no more to rise.
That treach'rous love, the mystery of man's life,
   Inglorious star to shine but for his god
And loving harlots—a neglected wife
   Will quench his light, e'en though it may seem odd :
On such great men, we mean the ignorant proud,
   God pours His vengeance just to give relief
To the empty prayers which they repeat so loud,
Whilst all their glory is beneath a cloud
   Of sickening smoke, till death comes, like a thief,
   To establish their own endless life of grief.
Such men, alas ! how many stars below,
   Whose lustful passions and deceitful heart
Soon bring to light the right deceiving foe,
Their Babel Towers will He not overthrow ?
   To solitude of gloom such quacks depart,
To live forgotten in a world of woe,
A just reward for such great stars of show,
They seek the glory of this world below.
Careless about cold death, or where they go,
To the darker regions, ah ! to show their light,
Among the unclaim'd dead, what sick'ning sight !
But what an end of such great stars so bright,
   To shine unnoticed in eternal gloom,
   In pain and sorrow far below the tomb !
November 5th, 1866.

THE CHURCHYARD.

WE contemplate, in solemn silent tread,
The churchyard scene, and read, with awful dread,
The records of our loving friends, the dead ;
We drop a tear, and think how sad to die,
And lift our hearts in pray'r to God on high,
Knowing that we soon shall join them here.
But Hope and Faith soon banishes the fear
Of death, and fills the heart with holy cheer ;
We see them, as it were, in joy and love ;
That inward eye of faith can see above,
Musing in the glory.   Oh ! to find
That comforting and holy peace of mind,
E'en in that quiet, silent tread
Of consecrated ground among the dead.

December 12th, 1862.

DEATH.

WE all await the coming of stern Death,
And soon, perchance, a few short days, alas !
May thus decide our fate in mortal life,
For all are travelling fast towards the grave.
How like a passing shadow !   Soon we're gone ;
Yea, all must go, to give account to Him
For all the sinful deeds concealed below,
In the light and presence of a just, good God.
    But let us rather hope to live and love
Each other in devotion of His light,

And thus be ready when the time shall come
To meet our God—to cheer each other home,
In the trackless path of life, eternal joy
Of never-ending day.

September 1st, 1864.

GOD WITH US.

CONSCIOUS of His presence,
The soul becomes awaken'd by great faith
Whilst feasting on His living light.   The truth's
Implanted in the heart, great joy to find
New life in God.
    'Tis only then the soul is lifted up :
The utterance of the tongue can equal not
Those solemn thoughts of joy-outpouring love.
(In adoration of Eternal God
Of smiling mercy) from a grateful heart,
Regarding not the world nor worldly things,
Man lives ; he cannot die ; his life is hid
In Him who is all Light, and Truth, and Love.

May 14th, 1868.

THE " INSPIRING VIRTUES " OF FRUITLESS TREES.

THE plane-tree, fine for beauty see ;
    What cares the rose a fig ?
Is there no balm in all Gilead
    For injuries done
    To such a one
Where fools cut down and dig ?

Ha, ha, degeneracy, what power !
They seek the fruit before the flower ;
The thorn and birch may give their shocks
 To make the elder bray ;—
  The myrtle box,
  But what's such knocks
 To keep the cork at bay ?
Ay, whilst the fir is far away,
In scanning Nature's works
 Of high and low degree ;
We sometimes find a tree of growth
Looking down upon the sloth
 In joyous mimicry :
Spontaneous droppings from the pine
Appear in language very fine ;
The sugar-cane and ginger-tree
 May for their good show pride,
For sweets and heats, but then the bees
 Find other trees beside ;
The fine bread-tree's fruition see,
The juicy apricot and peach
 Whilst green can speak out well ;
Although they cannot make a speech,
About their juices they can preach ;
But did you e'er know one teach,
 His exhaustless powers to tell ?—
When ripe, and may be out of reach
 The date on which he fell.

SENSITIVE QUACK.

AWFULLY-gloriously puffed up with pride—
Proud of his learning, undauntedly proud,
Discharging his "pop-guns" high in the air,
So full of exciting sensation matter,
To make more dreary the aqueous vapour
Of an unhealthy climate of perpetual
Extremes.   Laurels immortal encumber the head.
Such frenzy gives one a commiserative thrill,
Assuming the wisdom for glorious nothing,
Absorbing his shame ; ah, Sensitive Quack,
That changing of colour, that fugitive glance,
Is enough to outlaw any wretch in a trice,
For care-giving pleasure at still higher glory :
That public amusement of maddening sport :
Such virtues and honour regaled with small coals
Is the favour and taste of a seasonable " gent,"
So highly entertaining for learning and rank.
Well may the wise be so ready to burst
In jollity of laugh—but the biting the lip ;
Ah, censure suppressed, his virtue admitted,
No hostile feeling to dishonour his credit ;
The critic too harsh—the amusement is done,
The Quack underpaid for his reasonable fun ;
But where's the sport without rhyming skill ?
The sense must rhyme at other people's will.
How many think they're greater far than Milton,
By putting forth a little new-made Stilton !

And thus to show a perfect state of mind,
By fancy-dreams for glory so inclined.
There was, and is, perhaps, no cheaper way
To tell a man he's wise, but then I say,
Perchance should he in truth be such a fool,
Mistake your claret for thin water-gruel ;
Look grave, and tell him he's as full of light
As any other worldly star, as bright ;
'Tis then his changing colour may be seen
To change no more—remain a royal green.
Such living kindness crowns his happy days,
So puff'd and swollen by silly empty praise ;
He lives in darkness, nay, in fancy-light,
His social blessing, ah, a glorious sight,
An "eddicated" man so wronged of right !

THE VIOLET AND THE TULIP.

SWEET smiling Violet, why, why spread
Thy fragrance o'er the Tulip's bed,
Whose dying bloom falls on thy head
To hide thee as if thou wert dead ?
Unseen, unknown, hid from men's eyes,
Too meek, too charitable to rise
To pain the envious eye of bards—
Uneducated, quarrelsome " cards ;"
Affrighted, ay, what innocence
Of sympathising recompence.

Breathing odour just to keep
The dying Tulips out of sleep.
Well known for vulgar weeds, they live
To war with fragrant flowers.   To give
A death-blow should the Violet fair
Peep out to speak Forbear, Forbear—
What tyranny, what wrong, what care !

<hr />

THE LILY OF THE VALLEY AND THE TULIP.

VILLANOUS Tulip, why so courtly
    To thy kindred weeds ?
Why frown upon the Lily-blossom
    Of consecrated beads ?
Oh, live in peace ! Wouldst thou be fed
    By Lilies ?   Ah, take heed,
Lest their white blossom touch thy head,
Or simply kiss thy thick-lip red ;
    'Twould humble thee and bring thee low,
    Cause thee to search for weeds that grow,
    Or smaller flowers that only blow
And smile when thou art dead.
As Tulips only live for show,
So ignorant bards oft sing, you know,
" Do, Re, Mi, Fa, Sol. La, Si, Do."

SMALL TALK.

THAT " little knowledge," what's its good?
  Sometimes its power is odious,
The smallest star is understood,
  For light is weight commodious.
When greater stars of high degree
  Of magnitude retreat,
The smaller stars of light we see
  Are left alone to cheat,
Or outshine each other's light ;
For little knowledge has its right
  With equals to compete.

TO ———; FROM ———.

DEAR departed
Happy friend, thou art gone to thy last home,
Far beyond the reach of this world's sorrow,
In the holy light of eternal joy,
And living glory of thy loving God.
Ah, blessed friend ! though, alas ! thou art gone,
Unchangeable is thy angel-beauty,
Shining forth the very light of Heaven—
Divine enjoyment now eternally
Smiles on thy holy brow in Paradise.

THE GLORIOUS PASSING MONTHS.

Stop not, nay, continue on,
Fair June of declining beauty—yea, e'en in thy smiles
    pass on,
Tho' unwillingly we part with thee; ah! to lose thy
    charms.
How lovingly all things, in thy name, smilingly live to
    please us!
But though thy varied glorious beauty is now fast fading,
Pass on, pass on, O thou sweet month of beauty and
    song,
For thou'rt trembling under the weight of long spent
    loveliness,
And, alas, thou'rt become old! Ah, sweet age, pass on
    to take repose.
O that it may be as calm and sweet as thy life-giving joy!
Nature's warm sympathy gives the blessed signal
For July (that angel-month of timely, all-pitying tender-
    ness)
To come forth to relieve thee of thy burden,
And to lovingly caress thee in thy smiling departure.
                     Ah, fair, calm month,
But one short hour, and thy day is spent—life gone!
All thy sweet gentle givings e'en to bud and blossom
Will soon be in the light of another month.
Tho' the changing scenes are full of truth and beauty,
Yet, in the midst of life, how silently they vanish, to be
    no more!
Like man, who comes forth from the dust of the earth,

To live, and love, and die to be forgotten:
E'en so, like the blessed months of spring,
He comes and goes, as it were, in a midnight dream.

June 26th, 1861.

<hr>

GOD'S MERCIFUL LAW.

O THE divine perfection of His law,
The o'erruling wisdom of Providence,
The discipline of triumphant power,
In ev'ry moment of glorious time,
Calling forth beauty, light, and order
Out of deformity and confusion !
His works must live—His power's without limit,
The quenchless fire of o'erflowing glory,
Kindling in all things divine loveliness,
O how precious are the glorious beams
Of oriental sweet glowing delight,
Giving the joyous tinge of sacredness
To perfect the change when the eyelids close
In death—when the soul is carried away
By the gladdening streams of immortal pow'r
Of o'erflowing glory of ev'ry joy !
The new-born light of heavenly beauty
Lives for ever and ever.   All things
Invisibly exist, tho' they pass from us :
For the blended beauties of creation
Separate to unite in holier form,
To the glory of immortality—GOD'S LAW.

REFLECTIONS ON THE CHURCHYARD.

WHILST musing on the past, thoughts far away,
Conscience seems to speak ; I hear it say :
    " Read, mortal, and reflect ; beneath thy feet,
Here, in the churchyard, lie in mystery deep,
Side by side, both rich and poor in sleep,
Soon to awake their eternal doom to meet
In sorrow or in joy ; but do not weep,
The names of those inscribed upon the tomb
Are written in His light of power to shine ;
The holy ones as heav'nly flowers shall bloom
Again in smiling Truth so pure, divine,
E'en as the stars to shine."
    Behold the dead of glorious youth and age,
Brought here at last, their resting-place we find,
All men at last, the poet, priest and sage,
The wise and ignorant, not one left behind.
Oh, awful thought ! how soon to pass away—
A few short days, a little time to last,
Like the grass, to wither, die, decay,
We to our graves are travelling very fast.
    Come, sing His praise ; O Spirit, touch the chord,
The heart-strings of the soul's sweet tuneful lyre,
In joyous praise to glorify the Lord ;
O, Holy Spirit, come, our minds inspire.
The day soon spent—short time is given
To learn of God, and find our way to Heaven.
    Come, Holy Spirit, come before the dawn ;
Awaken all to prayer out of sleep,

And come to those who're yet unborn ;
Light up the world in holy glory deep,
Firmly fix thy spirit-working power
In every soul before that parting hour.
Quick flies the time in life ; soon man is gone,
Yea, loving friends one by one depart ;
And yet in endless light new joys are born
To counteract the sorrows of the heart.

Man whilst he lives is full of worldly care,
Yea, out of joy his very sorrows spring,
The morning flower at noon begins decay,
And yet new glories of delight still sing
His song of glory-praise from day to day.

"Build up " His Church, the pride of England's race,
That in the churchyard holy virtue trace
Its living worth of smiling heavenly grace ;
For father, mother, sister, brother dear,
The dearest, yea, the fondest, are brought here :
We meet a friend one day to look upon
In sacred friendship's dear familiar love ;
Another day scarce passed, alas ! he's gone.
We to regretful sorrow-tears are moved,
In prayer and hope to follow him above.

But what is man ?   His worldly riches fly ;
Yea, rich and poor, the beggar and the king,
Are on a level when they come to die.
Yet out of dust their " living good " shall spring.
Then let us live in light, and free from pride,
For in the sight of God man's humbled low ;
The beggar and the king now side by side,
Shall live again in endless joy or woe.

Despise no man, for see the Saviour's face
In him, the poorest—why not live to love ?
In being poor there can be no disgrace—
E'en the smallest may be raised to crowns above.
Then let us be what we pretend to be,
For false religion's fashion is a cheat—
That outward show in prayer of ostentation ;
Remember those, alas ! beneath our feet.
But true religion of the soul, how sweet !
Its light and truth is power of new creation.
    The time will come when all men shall unite
In holy love, in joyous strength delight
To serve One God, the giver of true light,
Of joys eternal, joy supremely given
To change the heart, and make man fit for Heaven !

FLOWERS AND WEEDS.

YE tiny emerald weeds, why bloom
    To cheer the insects' life ?
Do not they live to take up room,
    And cause much deadly strife ?
Flowers and weeds will disagree ;
    Each one would be divine,
    E'en without giving wine.
Why tempt the little working bee ?
'Tis not the prettiest flower d'ye see.
The uninvited weed in sight
Might e'en show a greater light ,
Than larger flowers of power and might.

The bee finds his own living bliss
    Sometimes in weeds that live to shine ;
'Tis only such he seeks to kiss
    That offers him most wine.

THE GLORIOUS MONTH OF JULY.

      HAPPY month !
Yea ! rapturous month of outspread glory,
    Of song-rejoicing power,
Sweet cheering summer smiles of light,
    And time-refreshing hour ;
The morning star of lustre bright,
The evening dew-kiss, sweet delight,
    The glorious genial shower ;
The midday sun's sweet holy beams,
The midnight shade in glory streams
    Of glowing, working love :
How full of praise and glorious light--
Sweet Nature's song of sweet delight
    Is breathed to Him above.
Our fields are crown'd—by God the Giver—
With plenty.   But where's thy prayer,
Oh man, for all these cherished gifts—
The corn, the fruit, and flower ?

M

THE POPULAR ACTOR.

SELF-HARMING
Creature of well-painted genius,
Of permanent beggary and daily fraud,
What indulgence—what splendid virtues,
Famed for worth—undistinguished merit,
Recognised for egotistic wit,
Elevated by that self-importance,
So captivating in genuine spirit—
Contemptuous cheerfulness of self-conceit,
So high above to outshine all the stars,
In expansive glory—oh, ludicrous folly
Of lofty littleness !

Mighty productive
Is that high-born glory so low in state
As to become the subject of perfection.
Exquisite madness of unlimited wisdom's
Inextinguishable light ascending fame—
How burdensome insipid is that greatness,
That blissful animated exalted glory,
Of unquestionable credit !

Ah, rude
Pretender, gloriously pitiful drudge !
That false condition—ah, revolving fate,
How full of strength-giving amusing pride,
Of unlimited flourishing beauty,
How rich in honour, yet how poor in state !
Ah, vulgar quality for taunting jeer,
From e'en lesser lights of appropriate fun,

Panting tumultuously in disgust,
To crown the actor with a pompous sneer,
Consigned to oblivion by supporting smile
Of common sense.

SPIRITUAL BLINDNESS.

SHALL we watch the enemies of His Church
The pernicious errors of the blind,
Gaining nothing more than living death
Under a cloud of eternal sorrow,
In the erroneous path of darkness,
Which leads to Hell?   Alas!
Not one ray of light can reach the soul
To give a glimpse of cheering hope in Hades—
For always dying and yet never dead
Are the enemies of eternal God.

BEAUTIFUL MAY.

1867.

WHAT holy grandeur!
Beautiful May,—yea, gloriously beautiful—
Heaven-born glowing animating objects
Smile in gladness, to cheer the mind
And soul of man.

     Thy awakened flowers
Of power and light expanding in their glory
Of unearthly beauty.
       Gloriously beautiful !
How fresh the glowing stars of brilliant light
Of diversified beauty !
       The woods and fields
How full of attractive grace and holy song !
The trees in flower—ah ! sign of timely fruit—
What promise ; oh, what hope ; what ruling love ;
What wondrous gifts !
       The flow'ry weeds,
The moss and beauteous grass o'erspread the earth—
Yea, everything below the stars of Heaven
Acclaim the praise of His creative hand,
Of living power.   What life and hope in God !

TO VANITY.

    INFANT toy,
Oh ! reckless folly of affectation,
Ruinous is thy deceptive vanity.
So much of self, that thy poisonous glory
Is hateful, indeed, as it becomes
Thy own victim !   Oh ! cursed be the hour
In which darkness had given thee power
To play upon the maddening brain of man.
In his slumber of glorious conceit.

"HAPPY NEW YEAR."

We wish
Friends (and foes if we have any)
A happy, prosperous year, and many
Glorious smiling joys on earth ;
To one and all that timely mirth
Which fills the soul with prayerful love
Of gratitude to Him above,
In holiness of light to dwell.
  From this time forth serve Him aright,—
So quit the world, but who can tell
  But ev'ry cross shall bring delight?
Rich and poor—each one a brother—
To serve his God and love each other,
That all may live and learn to die
To find new life in Him on high :
And thus in truth and faith to be
  One people in the light of day,
To be crown'd with joy eternity
  When Time himself shall pass away !

December, 1866.

BLESSED FAITH.

O, what is it but blessed profound faith
That secures the living hope in God,
Animates us e'en from the cradle to the grave,
Fills the soul with expectant spiritual joy,

Controls the faltering heart and treacherous mind,
And kindles within us that holy spark divine
To glorious living flame—Eternal Light,
That inward working change—O spiritual power?
And O, does not faith tell us—tell us this,—
That our very dear departed friends still live,
And that ere long we shall meet again
　　All those for whom our tears were shed?
　　Ah! fond remembrance of the living dead;
　　How can they be forgotten by us,
When we know they'll be raised from their mouldering dust?
Yea, for the soul and the body shall unite and come forth,
　　In humble state, before the throne
　　Of Him who calls all His own;
　　And loves to perfect ev'ry one,
　　Before that awful day.
But what is this world's blighted blossom—
O what is it?   Can we o'ercome the offspring of sin,
And be born again before our feeble light is out?
Nay, not without the blessed faith in God Jesus,
Which shines more and more until that perfect day.
Ah! faith indeed is the spirit of prayer,
And prayer the glory of all things.
Faith is that inward eye which beholds the invisible
Eternal living glory of God and Heaven.

LITTLE KINDNESSES.

In little kindnesses
The very poorest may do good ;
The least on earth can glad
The heart to cheer the soul of one
Oppress'd with burdens sad.
Yes ! one kind word may give new birth
To powers to fix a tear
Of gratitude for holy worth
In that which lifts him from the earth.
To chase away that deep-set care
Of ravishing despair.

HUMAN LIFE.

Soon we are gone !
Time is but a passing day
Of light to cheer us on our way.
Even to glorious Heaven.
Life's call'd forth from dust divine,
Its morning beauty how sublime !
Full of hope, yet quickening time
Consumes the gifts that's given.
The tears may trickle down the cheek,
The heart so full of sorrow—
Ha ! full of care, yet full of prayer,
In hope to meet in Heaven there
The departed one to-morrow.

April 25th.

TO-MORROW'S REPENTANCE.

WHEN the storm of life shall have passed away,
And the bright day of eternal glory
Of Almighty pow'r in joy shall triumph
Over Death, man may then see his error :
But not till then will he humble himself
To God in trembling fear and repentance—
When, alas ! too late for hope or mercy ;
For he prefers darkness to living light,
And so forfeits Heaven's o'erflowing joy
By obnoxious principles of dishonour—
E'en in the shadow of Death.
                              Blessed God,
Who can encounter this reality ?
Thy second coming to judge the world.
Not one of us is really holy, just,
Living in the incontrovertible
Truth and spiritual light of Heaven.

----•----

THE NEW YEAR.

ANOTHER year—just one more year is gone ;
The memory of the past brings painful tears
To ev'ry meekly loving Christian parent ;
Tho' the unwelcome messenger of Death
Replies in touching language, " All is mine "—
For he alone can find a resting place
To give serene repose and set man free :

Yet all is sorrow—ah ! yes, sorrow's given,
In loving smiles we see the living dead,
For in our wakeful thoughts and dreams of night
They're ever near, and though no shade is left
Of them on earth, they yet dwell in us
And live in God.   O love ! how strong indeed,
Stronger than death—yea, and far more precious
Is that glorious light for which man lives :
Ah, Light of Light, the very God of Love.
The sorrowful parting of a brother dear
Is the most difficult lesson Nature gives ;
For who can understand the living gone,
Whilst the glorious Sun night and day still smiles
To give us sweeter consolatory pow'r,
That we may meet the blessed in His light
Eternally to part no more ?   How glorious,
Yet how difficult to understand,
God's wonderful relationship to man.
Kind Providence, how blissful are thy charms
Of smiling grace and tender watchful pow'r,
Cheering the dying breath to quiet sleep,
Whispering wisdom, liberty, and love,
Sweet'ning ev'ry desponding thought of which
The troubled soul is burdened here
Whilst in the dust !   O Almighty Father
Of Heaven, how precious is that Light above
Which penetrates the heart to set man free !
Another year is gone—another come,
O that impending change, Life in Death !
Who can resist its mournful living pow'r

Of trembling tenderness, yet pitying joy,
Arising from the boundless depths of love?
Ah! God is near.   He speaks, His will is done!
All things obey.   But oh, unthinking man!
Not the mortal flesh can understand
The law which introduces ev'ry change
In the glorious pow'r and light of Heaven.

THE DAY'S SOON SPENT.

THE morning comes, and but a little while
     Its beauties smile :
Tho' in the meridian of its day all things are bless'd,
     By light caress'd,
Yet the day's soon spent, its glories pass away
     But to decay.
Yea, the hour of night soon closes with a smile
     Our earthly toil.
'Tis now at hand—we soon must go—beware!
     No time to spare.
Then serve the Living God, to gain His love
     In th' realms above!
Why should we careless be?—all pow'r is His
     Of life and bliss.
Where is the man who would not banish sin
     To enter in
The presence of his God, to love in light
     Of sweet delight?

Beware, alas ! for Death is drawing nigh—
                    Keep watchful eye
Upon the Lord : secure new life on high
                    Before ye die !
For O remember this—new joys are given
                    In light of Heaven.
Should we not strive that Holy One to see
                    In eternity ?
So make our calling sure in God, I say,
                    Whilst here we stay
That little time whilst Time itself rolls on,
                    For soon we're gone !

AUTUMN.

        CHARMING, beautiful autumn,
Season of delight—sweet cheering comfort !
Oh, how brief thy glorious life, and yet
How like a dream of perpetual joy,
Filling the heart with holy, thoughtful pray'r
As the falling leaves remind us of Death's
Vital change to the glory of God !
                    Beautiful autumn !
Can man forget thy sweet endearing smiles
As they vanish under the hour of winter ?
Though thy cheering flowers fade and droop,
As they breathe farewell to summer,
In lingering, dying smiles, they seek for rest,
But only such as winter-sleep can give.

Time cheerfully, ay, lovingly whispers,
Nature hath no destroying principle :
The vital energies of smiling beauty
Only sleep to awake again in pow'r
And ineffable glory to adorn
The future controlling, unerring spring.
Oh, fond memory of cherished beauty !
Can man forget the rapturous, bounteous
Gifts of autumn ?   How full of His glory
All things smile for the happy change in Death—
Glorious, blessed immortality !

October 8th, 1861.

———◆———

FEBRUARY.

January, thou'rt gone ! cold month, adieu !
Thy gloomy smiles indeed have died away :
Wert thou permitted to stay beyond thy time
Thou mightst indeed have made a barren waste.
The great Almighty Ruler called thee forth
In ruling evidence of past duration,
In the changing scenes which He ordains
For the good of man.   Farewell, farewell !
Linger thou couldst not ; time outsped thy course ;
Thou couldst not linger e'en in joy of love,
Whilst February is putting forth his strength
To show the beautiful flowers of earthly joy :—
The little violet now hath shown itself,

The primrose from repose will now awaken,
To gladden the heart of the beholder.
How changed the vision by these cheering objects !
Yea, all things in this onward course bespeak
A glorious prospect—for bright spring is nigh ;
Nature seems so full of tranquil glory,
In tenderness so glowing in its song,
In holy mirth so heav'nlike in its pow'r—
O glorious truths of exquisite delight !
Wisely indeed all things redound for good,
To cheer us in the precious passing moments.

SYMPATHY FOR THE SLOTHFUL.

SCORN not the form
Of a poor worm,
Nor crush its gloomy reign ;
But give it pow'r
To live an hour—
Hath God not will'd the same ?

A worm—little harmless thing !
No downy wings to spread,
To rise above its earthy bed.
To carry high its lowly head ;
But to earth and dust must cling,
Yet frantic birds delight to feed
Upon its shiver'd frame,

With courteous glance above the weed,
How full of grace the noble deed,
Seeking as the greatest need
A crawling insect, worm indeed !—
    There's magic in the very thought
      To satisfy the craw :
    The poor and slothful worm is caught
    Up by its feather'd friend and taught
      A lesson without law.

      Scorn not the form
      Of a poor worm :
    Its life by God was given,
      To live an hour
      In Nature's pow'r,
    In smiling light of Heaven.

GOOD NIGHT.

Hush! child, sleep and take thy rest
Upon a loving mother's breast ;
Thy lisping pray'r of holy love
Will bring down pity from above.
"My darling child," the mother said,
"I hear the Angel's silent tread ;
God claims the little one His own,—
Ah, dearest, thou'rt not alone ;
Oh, close thine eyes in holy rest
Upon a loving mother's breast.

Good night, good night! oh, warm embrace,
Let mother kiss thy angel face!
Once more good night, sweet child of love,
O take thy rest and sleep in God."
The gentle mother, with fix'd eye,
In pray'r to Him who dwells on high,
At once exclaims in tones so sweet,
" Is Jesus come my child to greet ?"
The infant, sleeping on her breast,
In song and pray'r to God is bless'd ;
Peace on its brow, sweet joyous light,
Ah, holy love, supreme delight!
For these enchanting words "Good night"
Is poetry in its heav'nly light :—
There's music in its melting tone,
When mothers speak it to their own.

WHY WAS HE BORN?

MAN for holiness was born,
   But only for that cause,
To live and glorify the Lord
   And to obey His laws:
      To live amongst the wisely proud,
         The empty-headed weak,
      Who only live to boast aloud,
         Yet know not what they speak.

Man to troubles here was born—
  The world, alas! to hate ;
To hail and watch the coming morn
  To crown his happy fate:—
    From the cradle to the grave
      He lives midst love and strife—
    Friends to cheer and foes to mar
    His joys, to shorten life.

Man for holiness was born—
  To breathe his power of love,
So to conquer sin and death
  For endless joys above.
    Soon in death, alas! to hear
      The solemn call to Heaven—
    Faith and hope in light to cheer
    Eternal joy that's given:
To fill the soul with endless bliss
And find in that true happiness.

May 27th, 1867.

THE STARS OF HEAVEN.

O ye immortal stars of living light,
Delighting in His infinite Wisdom's
Inimitable glorious beauty,
Plainly ye speak the wondrous works
Of the Most High God and Eternity.

O ye beautiful stars of holiness,
Immeasurable is the mighty glory,
The heav'nly encircled living Light
                    Of Almighty God.

September 11*th*, 1861.

BACKBITING IN THE "BACK SLUMS."

"COURTING COUPLE."

                    THEY say so :—
That Mrs. So-and-So says so ;
But everybody ought to know;
And so they progress through the day,
Till every neighbour has to say
What Mrs. So-and-So has said
    Out of envy, or of spite,
    Gossiping from morn till night
In every cottage-shed.
        What do they say
        Day after day ?
What matters ? let them talk away ;
But so-and-so—ah, well, they say,
Because Jill frowns why should Jack shun
    His talking "gal?"—who plainly hints
That spoony looks create more fun
Than brighter fools when two make one,
    And that bright booby only squints :
For Mrs. So-and-So says so,
And everybody ought to know.

N

But poverty and idleness
Is some poor creatures' happiness ;
Tho' what the dames say is so shocking,
That each has neither shoe nor stocking,
And yet there is that horrid rocking ;
Ha ! but they deserve a "whacking,"
For enthusiastic smacking,
For Mrs. So-and-So says so,
What everybody ought to know.

September 9th, 1870.

"BLESSED ARE THE POOR."

THE rich are sent to clothe the naked poor,
To cheer and feed the hungry, and instruct
In wisdom's path the downcast, and to show
By good examples godlike living care,
Free from inglorious prejudice and pride,
The way in holiness to life above.
Rich and poor as one beyond the grave—
The poorest brother has a soul to save.

DERISION.

THO' trifles vex, yet smaller things may please
The scornful fool to contemptuous laughter,
Just to show the fury of his madness ;
As did Goliah, when he met David,
Coolly arrange himself to be despatched
In his bantering stage of mania.

GLORIOUS SUMMER.

In the light of summer
Everything that meets the eye
 Instructs and elevates the mind,
Lifts man's soul in prayer on high,
 New unseen glories yet to find.
By faith that holier joy in truth is given
To cheer the heart in th' immortal light of Heaven.
 Farewell, bright spring ;
Adieu, O season of delight ;
 Depart in joy of song,
In Nature's glory power of light;
 We would thy stay prolong.
E'en now in summer's glorious morning smile
Canst thou not stay beyond thy time awhile ?
 Not so, alas ! for spring must sleep,
In answering tone of Nature-youth ;
 The awak'ning summer " time-watch " keep
Revealing glories of her truth.
For in the changing seasons summer comes to bring
Forth ripening fruit of trees that bloomed in spring.
 O, now the summer's golden gifts appear !
 Welcome summer, full of life and beauty !
In Nature's power the seasons of the year
 Come and go in smiling light of duty.
In the brightness of their time they pass away,
In glowing joy of hope returning day.

JUNE.

O LET us direct our thoughts and prayers to God on high
For this most bounteous supply of June's bright golden gems,
That are kissed by the gentle dewdrops in the morning sun ;
The genial warmth awakening and rekindling
The lingering fading flowers to refreshing beauty,
Whilst Nature—ah ! emulating Nature's pow'r—
Is bidding the smallest, tenderest buds unfold
Their invisible, startling bloom of infant beauty.
How welcomely cheering ! O how beautiful are all things !
The smallest and meanest object on earth is in God's favour !
In His keeping, ever loved and blessed,
As they adore Him in the language-song of Heaven:
The birds rise high on quivering wing to sing
The songs of praise for that indulgent liberty
Which is so dear—so precious to all created beings
That live and move under His guardian care;
The mingling sounds of answering songs below
Of the never-weary winged and wingless insects—
How full of glory they seem! O how lovely to behold
These almost hidden wonders to man! God's holy work,
So mysteriously and wonderfully shaped for life and duty :
Watch them with spirit-eyes, skipping to kiss their shadow
Under every tiny weed and flow'r that cover the land.
How full of beauty-breathing spirit are all things,
So wisely ordained—chaste philosophy— God's glory!
Oh! mark the beauty—living varied beauty—
Of the dissolving views of the passing months,
As they venture on in turn and smilingly vanish,

Bidding man keep steady, watchful eye
Whilst Creation's Spirit reveals the prime of spring:
Oh! that Divine, inconceivable, impressive power;
That Holy Spirit of heavenly eternal goodness—
Wisdom's immortal glorious trust and duty!
Oh! this teaching—this elevating the soul to amazing worth—
Speaks the matchless love of the living God;
All things speak His inestimable power.
How full of sublimities and Divine truths
Is this month of June! Ah! blessed month
Of vital spark—restless power giving beauty.
Nature's inspired givings are wonderful indeed ;
Out of unsightly, shapeless, solitary, cold clay
Spring forth incessantly incomparable beauty and glory !
Ah! there is that godlike soul in all things—
The germ—the smallest seeds are touched with power!
Power-giving task to come forth to beauty, and ripen
All things, though so far beyond the comprehension of man.
Understand the wonderful teaching of Him
Who speaks the word, and His glorious will is done.

June 4th, 1861.

CONTINUE IN PRAYER.

COL. IV., 2.

O THAT supreme pleasure of the mind,
When the whole heart in pray'r is given to God,
In that Divine principle the Light of Truth,
Which shines more and more in holy beauty,

Freeing the soul of its worldly sorrows,
E'en unto death giving eternal life
And glory !
                Does not the great Author God
Claim our adoration ?   How delightful
The task, man learning to live for Heaven !
O let us look up in pray'r and rejoice
In the blessed hope of immortality.
O that transition of sorrow to joy—
Death, ah, Death swallowed up in victory !
But, O man, nothing but lasting glory
Can be found in the light of the living good ;
The unsearchable riches of Heaven
Are found in holy prayer of faith and love.
O Spirit of light ! O Spirit of joy !
Not quite certain are we of His goodness
Uplifting man from dust to life and glory.
Spirit Divine imparting holy Light,
Touch'd by the living pow'r the wondrous mind
Becomes acquainted with the living God,
Who made man to His glory and for Heav'n ;
And so man lives in cheerful thoughts of Him
Whose will is that an angel he become
By holy pray'r in holy faith and love,
To live for ever with the saints above.

GAIN A LOSS.

"ALL flesh is as grass." 'Tis truly said,
By ambition man gets over-heated,
As the firing of hay when stack'd too green—
The last appearance in that primitive state,
On barren land ; elevated regions
Becoming inflated by its rotten ripeness :
Such gain is loss, unfit for use it dies
By its own annihilating power,
Combined with perfect horror in conjunction
With the unhappy sympathising tiller,
Whose parental care had rear'd for better use,
For higher rank, the object of his choice.
But ah, by length of time man's often hid
From early credit by his rapid growth
Of torpid ignorance in early culture.

MARCH.

BLEST, happy,
Glorious March, of life-inspiring hope,
How full of holy mystery is thy life—
Smiling in the light of living joy,
Of song and beauty !   In Nature's smile
How gladsome is thy ruling lawful pow'r
To cheer the eye with overflowing gifts—
The woodland, fields, and every lawn-like spot,
Mantled with thy spangled, glowing stars

Of streaming light, glorying in the birth
Of innocence and joyous smiling beauty,
To cheer the earth and teach man how to live
In adoration of eternal God !

THE TATTLING KNAVE.

THE self-convicted petty quack,
  Of power-working gladness,
Who makes his house a scandal-shop,
  By his libellous madness,
Which only shows the serpent-guile
In his falsifying smile.

But, as a two-faced tattling knave,
  Of vulgar, sickening pride,
He's coaxed and fed by every fool—
  His rights are not denied,
For such unbidden folly-fun
Is recognised by every one.

His liberal state of happy fate,
  His glory-light, he fears
Can never show his learning great,
  Unless he clips his ears—
Such sacrifice, alas ! is seen
To be too cruel or too mean.

CHRISTMAS IS NIGH.

TIME passes on—how fast the moments fly !
The Holy Star is rising in the East,
To show his glorious splendour in the sky.
Oh, messenger of life, and love, and victory !
Man shall sing thy praise.

How full of lovely toil and smiling joy !
How sweet the melody of Nature's song !
Ha, glorious is the light of heav'nly hope,
Gleaming forth that universal praise
Of provident goodness.

Christmas
Is nigh, yea, joyous holy Christmas
Of new-born happiness—oh, sweet delight,
Exulting in the living law of light !
Sweet loveliness Divine to charm the heart
Of man, e'en in the rise and sunset
Of life.

How glorious is His law and pow'r,
In the light of Jesus Christ our King,
Who lived and died to give man peace on earth—
E'en to a Father's joy, that he
Might live again, eternally above,
In heavenly felicity.

THE TREE OF LIFE.

MAN must be roused to solemn awe
And cautious fear, impatient to serve God,
When he beholds with truthful eye
That heavenly reasoning power—the Tree of Life–
Silently putting forth in one short dream,
In godly fancy, its hidden sacred treasure.
The bloom—the living bloom of the glorious tints of heaven,
Designed for what ?—for liberty, love, and eternal beauty ;
Its blessed branches are enshrined in imperishable goodness,
Caressed in the awakening passion to heavenly sentiment
Which is ever in Divine truth—the very light
That illustrates the power and the fruit of the living soul,
On which the name of God is most mysteriously inscribed.
There is that approaching beauty and heavenly innocence
Which bespeak the wisdom, power of the Almighty Hand,
When the tender buds of heavenly-ting'd beauty shoot forth,
So full of smiling liberty, light-living light,
Watching the secret signals of the parent-stem
To unfold that invisible unknown living glory
Which belongs only to Christ Jesus, the living God.
O, that infinite power ! this task—this reckoning with Him,
Whose works are indeed so wonderful, sublime, and complete,
Nourished by God—ah ! but where momentary absence
Would cause instant confusion, death, and ruin.
But this Tree of Life can never die ; 'tis of heavenly growth ;
Its sacred branches spread so far and wide
Beyond the shadow of Death and this world's glory !

THE SECOND MONTH OF THE YEAR.

THE days now lengthen, and the early flowers
    Seem to awaken out of winter-sleep,
To gladden man e'en in his hopeful hours ;
    But watch their glory as they smile to peep
Out from beneath the leaves in truthful mirth—
What joyous beauties springing from the earth.

Sweet February—month of golden prime—
    Imparting to repay, by silent deeds,
An equal blessing in His light divine
    On smiling, fragrant flowers and rankest weeds.

Thou blissful month of lofty truth sublime,
    What poetry of superseding power
Is found in thy sweet life-restoring time,
    The secret joy of ev'ry opening flower !

CHRISTMAS DAY.

WHILST feasting in delight, what can one know
    About the sickly, starving, suff'ring poor,
Whose swollen eyes now force the tears to flow ?
Ha ! so soon to close from this sad world below
Of cold neglect—what wretchedness and woe !
Oh, Charity ! alas, behold the sight,
    Gather up the fragments, go and see
That Holy One who blessed the widow's mite.
    Thou'lt find Him in the midst of poverty,

Smiling forth His light upon the poor
(E'en whilst the holy angels guard the door).
Oh, see His look for timely help that's given,
    The soul revived by holy Christmas cheer.
The helping friend shall find reward in Heaven
    For lifting up a starving brother here,
In smiles of Him who cometh from above,
    To bless this day of feasting and delight,
And lead us all to holiness above
    In glory-joy of never-ending light.

THE GLORIOUS CATHOLIC CHURCH.

    In His Church " the administering
Help " is in the name of our true God ;
And by that power, and in His holy love,
Man's lifted in the light of Heaven above—
Gloriously crown'd in majesty and grace,
In lofty pow'r to behold his Saviour's face.
Glorious, yea, unspeakably glorious power
Is given till that solemn " parting hour,"
In the hour of death, that sweet calm-giving rest—
O the " living dead," immortalised and blest.

His glorious Church of spirit-giving light.
The way, the life, God's word of truth and love ;
In meditating power of sweet delight,
Man's carried by his faith to Him above.

There is but *one* true living Church on earth :
Oh may His Spirit guide us while
We see the light of truth, e'en from our birth,
To live in love and grace of His sweet smile !

Man may dissent, and set up his false God
For earthly gain, for worldly glory live ;
Still one and all must bow beneath His rod,
And come to His " true Church " at last, to give
Their praise and glory to its power and Head,
The Saviour.   Ha ! the Apostles who have bled !
We in the footprints of the Saints of Heaven
Must walk, by faith and prayer to be forgiven,
As pilgrims journeying in the light that's given.

―――――――

PARADOXICAL.

NONE happens to know the great man of research,
Who's seldom at home, but never at Church.
We pity the *lame*, ah, because *he* must own
As *he's never seen out he* can *never* be *known*.

GREAT "STARS."

POETS of course may smoke if in a crowd
　　Among great men, who puff away at will,
To show their rising glory in a cloud;
'Tho' dirty pipes ne'er are allow'd,
　　Unless the colouring show superior skill.

———◆———

"RISING GLORY."

YE swelling Northgate-birds, why prone
　　To pick up worms in frantic rage,
Whilst smaller birds on crumbs alone
　　Live for the prison-house or cage?
See that tall man whitewashed on bail,
　　So, *honest like*, has nought to give;
Would throw salt on a small bird's tail,
　　Or let a little sparrow live.
If doing business means a fail,
　　So that small creditors may win,
Then have your cash down on the nail,
　　And claim protection for your *tin*.

———◆———

THE KEYNOTE OF MATRIMONY.

THE pinchbeck may be thought the best ;
  Its properties may shine ;
Nay, cut a dash without the aid
Of gold or silver, I'm afraid—
  Its metal power's divine.

Bell metal may be very well,
  Its glorious ring may charm,
But 'tis the tin that makes the belle,
And gives that high-note sounding swell
  That causes the alarm.

DOUBLE FACE.

WHAT can be, oh ! more sick'ning than the smile
  Of him whose tongue (oh pestilential breath !)
Speaks to deceive, the virtuous to beguile
  By honey-words with poison mixed for death.

PUFF'D UP, SELF-RIGHTEOUS, PROUD : THE ELECT.

          IN her thin winding-sheet,
Poor ignorant creature—ah, but who can trust
  Such pride in vain display, what pomp and show !
The sixteenth verse, the sixth of Matthew, must
  Point her reward, and send her down below,
  Where but the self-righteous have a right to go.

APRIL.

SMILING April, gay and free—
    Welcome is thy cheering birth ;
    Spread thy glories o'er the earth.
Joyous stars of mystery
    In their purity all shine,
Glorify their Maker—see
    Their animating joy divine,
Teaching the adorative mind
To seek by constant pray'r, to find
    The light that smiles eternally
To show the way, in time that's given,
To holiness—the joy of Heaven.

April 2nd, 1867.

"HERE SHE COMES."

HERE she comes,
Tiptoe, smiling, fairy beauty ;
    Little star, what love to trace !
'Tis a joyous holy duty
    Just to kiss that angel-face.
Infant angel, gem of love,
    God will bless, and even give
Smiling, glory-light above,
    Holiness in joy to live.

Yes, I love that angel-beauty
  Full of living worth and joy,
In the light of holy duty,
  Every blessing to enjoy;
Here on earth, above on high,
Such a one can never die.

November 26*th*, 1866.

THE OLD AND THE NEW YEAR.

ALAS! Old Year, thy life-declining power
  Is well-nigh spent, and thou must pass away;
Peace be to thee in thy last dying hour
  Of measured time. Alas! then, wouldst thou stay
  When all thy gifts in nature speak decay?

Pass on, Old Year, in praises of the earth,
  To find that change in peace. Art thou not blest
By Time himself, who's watching to give birth
  To that New Year which shall soon give thee rest,
And glorify in light of holy truth
The new creations of eternal truth?
Awake! arise! to cheer throughout the land,
  To welcome in the New and happy Year.
"Tis by the power of His Almighty hand
  That life and death and changes take place here
To teach us how to live (whilst toiling on),
  And thus improve the time and chance that's given.
Before another year we may be gone,
  And who shall say that he is fit for Heaven?

O

TO CHARITY.

WISE Charity—
Heaven smiles approval of thy love :
   God blesses thee, the blest :
Ha ! workest thou to do His will
   Before thy sleep of rest ?
When thy final moments come
   Thy soul shall then rejoice,
For kindness—O thy happy doom,
   When thou hear'st His call and voice :
" Come thou blessed, come to Me,
   Into thy joy of light,
Behold the riches, come and see
   Thy holy gifts delight,
Which thou hast given, yea, to mine,
   The poor that walk'd the earth ;
Come take thy blissful fill divine,
   The joys of heavenly birth.
Boundless treasures are in store
   For thee who lived for love ;
Ten thousand blessings, yea, and more,
   A crown of life above,
Awaiting thee, blest Charity.—
   Come to thy home of light.
Of living joy eternity—
   Of holiness delight."

WHAT IS MADNESS?

Who but the prudent insane
Would covet the coronet of black diamonds?
Who but the sensitive madman would covet popularity,
Just to be taunted, envied, and cruelly despised—
Undeservedly censured, of course
By underhand prejudices of an enlightened people?
The serpent-ambition of uneasiness creeps into the soul,
To kill the golden grains of hope and knowledge—
That refined emotional pow'r of diamond beauty,
Altering that lovely form of man—image of God,
That was created for light and truth to shine for Heaven.
Who but the unstable, fickle, earnest insane
Would attempt to build castles in the air,
When so many apartments are to be let up there
By the encouraging people of unmistakened zeal?
Sober piety—milk-and-water benevolence of £ s. d.
Who but the very learned insane of unclipped wings—
Of high-born notions, of commanding authority and dignity,
Would be thus animated by vain glory above?
    In exalted happiness just to cut a dash.
    Threatening all below with mighty fearful splash.
Ah, they covet the cheese, and lose the living bread,
But 'tis cheese that generates the mighty power
    When strong enough to take effect, you know,
    To correspond with other things below.
Though honest truth is full of rhyming beauty,
    Yet cheese when strong and " mity" gifted
    Only rhymes with small coals sifted.

So great individuals crown the greatest errors;
They elevate a brother to the skies;
For out of mud-traps thus we're puffed up,
    Filled with transport-bliss till overcome
    By common-sense, which smiles at the fun.
Who would be crowned with this free-giving glory?
Dreadful sentence of transporting bliss,
On a desolate barren land of thorns and thistles,
No one, we think, but a gorilla of gentle blood;
Tho' every one have particular crotchets to spend,
Yet all would not be claret wine that could,
For strength above the proof may be regretted—
    " The Saviour through benevolence divine
    For festive mirth turned water into wine;
    Could the ' little fish ' arrange the matter
    They'd turn again that wine to water."

    July 16th, 1861.

THOUGHTS ON THE GRAVE.

How many in the churchyard lie,
    Their souls perchance in ecstasy,
    Crowned in glorious majesty,
In living light on high !

Yea, many in the churchyard lie,
    But are their souls in grief above?
We contemplate, reflect and sigh.
In hope and prayer until we die.

All live in ceaseless love,
In mental joy of holiness,
Crowned in heav'nly blessedness,
To all eternity.

June 7th, 1865.

THE DEATH-HOUR-GLASS.

THE sand
In the death-hour-glass is running fast,
And the light of the day is nigh spent,
Tho' the spark that lights up the power of the soul
May be losing its brightness on earth,
To pass on more brilliant in holy control
To the Giver, by whom it was sent.
Not an atom is lost in life's primitive pow'r—
'Tis a pow'r so divine in its light—
Watch the tender sweet bud expanding to flower,
Then to vanish from the world in delight :
Still the same glowing pow'r in another form lived,
For the hour of death is the giving of breath—
Man's life, so to speak, begins at his death.

Homeward bound we all are to the world afar :
Short-liv'd—we all know we must die,
This dark world to leave, up to inhabit a star
More gloriously beautiful on high.

Then, let us in love, before the "death-call,"
Hold counsel—great God, be all praised!
As in Adam all die—yea, all men must fall—
Yet, through Christ we all hope to be raised.

MARCH.

DELIGHTFUL month of opening bud and dignified grandeur,
So full of flow'ry gems of godly purity and loveliness—
Countless and beautiful as the stars of heaven,
Beautiful indeed, so full of mirth and light,
To please the eye and gladden the heart of man,
Influencing him to think more of his Maker,
Whose works, tho' unchangeable, are past finding out.
Blessed works! full of smiles, O how sweet the memory!
But alas! each individual hath a different scene;
Happy, or unhappy, is man in his vision;
Life indeed is but a glorious dream.
Delightful month, how very blessed thou art!
The singing of the birds midst thick-set branches
In the shady ivy-mantled trees,
The humming of the bee from flower to flower,
In every lawn-like place there's growing beauty,
Flowery weeds, and flowers of varied hue,
Yielding instruction, delight. But glory to Him
Whose power, mercy, and goodness are for man.
O may he learn to think—prayerfully think
All these great blessings flow for him alone!

March, 1861.

THE HYPOCRITE.

"A hypocrite, if we carefully attend to his behaviour, will be found to perform the exterior duties of virtue in a manner very different from those who discharge them through real principle."—*The Military Cabinet*, vol. ii., p. 224.

To man
It matters not who acts the hypocrite—
Not he ; but God alone can judge a brother
Who cheats himself, thriving in his sin,
As the champion of falsehood labouring
To deface the image of his Maker :—
Under the fearful wrath of His displeasure,
He suffers man to live in false devotion
'Till death shall take him in his fallen strength ;
Then the fiery darts of indignation
Shall fall from Heaven to wound the honour
Of the dissembler.   For then, oh, alas !
He shall partake of Hell's tormenting flame.
Then, and not till then, shall he be known
(To man) as an enemy to himself
And God.

REVENGE.

MALEVOLENT spirit of vengeful wrath,
Exulting in the strength of dismal dross,
And self-deceiving inexorable fraud ;
Draw back thy sting of sharp tormenting pow'r
To slaughter.

How keenly sensibly felt
Is the iteration of insatiate
Hate and revenge !

Dark dread; oh ! agony,
The scorpion stings of fiery indignation,
As piercing arrows from the fount of poison,
Thirsting for blood in delight of furious
Madness—in contempt of God for victory.
Oh ! arbitrary ruler of the bottomless pit,
Thou shalt have thy day of eternal sorrow,
When thy victims shall be bless'd for evermore.
But stop, canst thou not grow a little wiser ?
Ah ! no, for thy infamy's innate :
Thy daring caresses in the mournful brawl
Of thy death-call song, oh ! immodest cheat,
Will soon be o'er.

For, murderous prince—
Ah ! sinful monster of eternal darkness—
The critic's penetrating eye is on thee,
To overthrow thy hellish crew and kingdom,
By the light of spiritual love and virtue—
That divine knowledge of triumphant glory,
Given by God to overcome the foe,
In the latent battle of revenge.

April 24th, 1862.

WORLDLY RICHES.

WHAT are riches, clothed in withered leaves,
When their direful cank'ring sting of glory
Blinds the spiritual eye to wound the soul !
What are they in the eyes of the dying sick,
Eclipsed by sorrow and in pain forgotten !
O what are they in this life's coming end :
A mere shadow in mortality's hill !
            And yet
These worldly gifts entrusted to man's care,
Dedicated to God's holy purpose
Alone, advance to glory hereafter.

"THE SONG OF THE POOR CURATE."

You say "your spoon is pewter,
   Your cup is made of wood,"
That some say "a poor tutor
   Should have nothing that's good."
Why should a man of parts
   Not starve ?   Alas ! I say,
There's very few kind hearts,
   Until one faints away,
   Would raise a tutor's pay.
He may endear himself—
   A thief's affection win,
Who would do more with pelf
To make a "golden calf"—

Would he invite him in
To steal his " pewter," ay,
  To return its weight in *tin*,
And so get double pay.
His wooden cup, I say,
He might then throw away,
Yet learn to live and pray—
  In danger he might sit,
    In peril he might kneel ;
  He must not care a whit
    If " thieves break through and steal."

THE ENLIGHTENED GREAT OF NO MIND.

COLENSO hath no appetite
  For the truth of His Word as a guide,
Tho' the bishop's a man so polite—
Whilst Moses now stands in his light ;
He'd burn the first book if he might,
  Just to see the more clear his own pride.
Whilst the good-natured world who're so blind
Would doubt not a saint so refined—
  Yet the wise have no time to deride
The enlightened man who's no mind.

December 27th, 1866.

WHY MOURN?

Oh why should the soul be so disquieted,
The mind tormented, mourning ev'ry loss
Of worldly gain ? Does not eternity
Demand all things of death, the faithful giver
Which Providence ordains ? Then why, alas !
Does the heart fail, sickening in its grief
Midst hope and dread of immortality ?

POLICE.

The Police are energetic men,
Though often find abuse ; but then
They have a virtue (that can save
Them from the persecuting slave) :
Their reason guides them to be grave,
Yet faithful, loving, firm, and brave,
To fix suspicion on the knave
And other *honest* men : to stop
To catch the "lame ones on the hop "—
Those who partake of sin and vice,
E'en those who are not over-nice,
That give and take with thieves alone,
Or those who do not know their own.
    The Police, ah, let us then protect,
As mutual friends in turn respect,
And pay them well (but here's the beauty
In seeing that each does his duty,

And not to overstep his bounds
To find "dishonour" in his rounds).
We know they are but human creatures,
But then we want good moral teachers :
We do not wish to be their preachers,
But should one be upon the "hop,"
'Tis then high time, we think, to stop
His sovereign power, or further claim,
Expel him and blot out his name,
So brand the fellow's face with shame.

September 12th, 1870.

A LESSON OF NATURE.

PAUSE but a moment ere thou crush that worm,
   For wouldst thou rob the bird of his live bait?
Doth not fair Nature bid thee live and learn
(That thou may'st want some pity in return)
   That lesson, thou shouldst leave things to their fate ?
   Kill nothing here that thou canst not create.

September 13th, 1870.

THE ODD MAN.

MUTTER'D Jack to his wife :
   " I am tired of my life,
And sick of my miserable wealth ;"
   Replies wife to poor Jack :
   " There are two things you lack,
And they are contentment and health."

Says Jack : " I have health,
And my miserable wealth
Is *you*, my sweet pet, my own jewel ;
I'd quarrel for my right,
But I'd fall in the fight,
Where's my gun ?—let me fight my own duel."

September 13th, 1870.

"RESPECTABLE SINNERS ;"

OR, DIRTY-WHITE SHEEP.

APART from human black sheep,
These dirty-white ones out beyond their fold
  Go far astray, but to become still bolder
To wander on to find the " calf of gold "—
  To gain their independence from the rest ;
  To show by " virtue " how they can be blest ;
  To run alone, and e'en become still bolder,
  And in good time to offer the cold shoulder
To those who had them in their righteous keeping—
Blest holy guides that are now left a-weeping
For those ungrateful " white sheep " of the Church
For leaving their good teachers in the lurch.

September 12th, 1870.

TO A TOAD.

[On seeing one in a cucumber-bed watching for its prey.]

THERE'S nought on earth below the sky
More beauteous than thy glowing eye ;
   Thy reptile form, yet so displeasing—
Well may'st thou hide* thyself.   (Oh fie !)
Almost from view thou canst rely
On each unguarded silly fly ;
For not an insect passes by
   Thy hungry jaws that's so deceiving.

September 13*th*, 1870.

THE VIOLET, PRIMROSE, AND SNOWDROP.

FAIR and beautifully bright
   Smiles the Violet blue ;
Mark the Primrose in delight,
And the Snowdrop's living light,
Pure and holy, spotless white,
'Teaching man to see aright
   The hand of God how true
In Nature's law creative power—
   Yea, mark the pow'r that's given,
Behold the progress of each flower,
   The quick'ning light of Heaven.

---

* The only thing that could be seen of the toad was its open
mouth, into which insects crawl.

KING TULIP.

A MASCULINE Tulip in gorgeous array
Looked down in contemptuous scorn
On a meek little Violet, the glory of day,
Peeping out in the smiles of the morn.
Said the Tulip to Violet, in pride-making power,
" Were it not for my light, thou mean-looking flower,
Thou couldst not have come forth by sun or by shower."
" Ha, ha," said the Violet, " perhaps, my good friend,
You'll excuse no resentment—how could I offend ?"
But to cheer the small weeds, she good-naturedly said,
" Were it not for *their* fragrance *we* might have been dead."
Let us glory and praise such a great monarch born
That he above all should attract and adorn.
Does he live, aye to show his fine scarlet-lip bloom,
Unconscious of feeding on Violet perfume ;
Revived by inferiors, thou king of great powers,
The weed thy superior in language of flowers ?
Ah, thou the most mighty for goodness—but why ?
Were it not for thy glory small flowers would die ;
Self-importance, alas ! can never disgrace—
Little things for small minds are ne'er out of place—
So barren. Why flatter, ye weeds, your great king ?
The most quarrelsome monarch, the pride of the ring—
Contending for power, yea, in winter and spring,
Whilst insects rejoice and singing-birds sing
To crown the King Tulip—great honours to bring.

FIRST OF MAY.

DAY FOR SENTIMENTAL SWEEPS OF OBSCURITY.

How sublime
That sentimental beauty in disguise !
   Poetic language of the obscure race ;
'The cry of " Sweep ! " to sell his soot to rise,
   And strike the bargain with a blacken'd face.
But such romancing often turns a joke
When fortune's really gain'd by smoke ;
There are patronizers always to be found
Who pat the back of ev'ry learned clown,
Worthy of his hire—there's room for all,
Tho' many in the scrape may get a fall,
E'en by their borrowed light to get a state,
They do repay the debt, to personate
The real sweep so recognised and lost;
But who's to pay the piper for such cost ?
Let such a one consume his smoke and fear
No drawback from a brightened atmosphere.
The sun, with all his splendour, to delight,
Will show upon the darkest object light :
That is, alas ! when one shall gain his right,
To crown his truth that black is sometimes white.
But now the moments fly to make us gay,
The " good time's coming " on the first of May :
How many blacks in white on that fair day
Dress up to crown their glory on full pay ?

LANGUAGE OF FLOWERS.

FLOWERS indeed of holy light
  And ev'ry leaf hath got a trust ;
Ten thousand tongues speak His delight,
  And praise Him as they rise from dust.

On ground unhallowed but to God,
To consecrate the living sod
From which they rise to speak His name,
  In meek submission to His will,
They bow their heads to sleep again,
  The law of Nature to fulfil.

And so it is with man on earth,
  Call'd by Nature into light
To serve his God, e'en from his birth,
  In holiness of pure delight ;
To live and grow in perfect grace
  In faith and prayer till he in love
Can recognise His holy face—
  His Maker, Father, God above.

P

"A SONG FOR MAY."

"Shout, shout, a welcome out, for May the garland weaver."

"FLOWERS" that charm with colours bright,
  If found beneath the sod,
      May have a trust
      In crumbling dust
  To purify and set us right :
    Mark their perfumes. how odd !

Ask that wise man what makes his gladness ?
Will he reply to show his madness ?
    Tell us his yellows might be greens.
  His "garland-weavers" a delusion ;
  But then his mind was all confusion—
    'Tis *flowers of sulphur* what he means.

FLOWERS AMONG THE TOMBS.

WELCOME ye shades of endearing beauty—
    O ! sacred garden of rest,
Exulting in glory of heavenly duty,
    Sweet flowers eternally blest :
Kissed by the stars—-oh ! rapturous touch—
    The dewdrop's fresh'ning power ;
E'en angels of joy would envy such,
    For His light is in ev'ry flower.

Welcome, ye shades of sacred rest,
　Ye flowers of heavenly duty,
Smiling in innocence tenderly blest,
　Expanding to glorious beauty.
Ye smile for the dead, the living dead,
　In that heavenly garden of rest,
To glory and praise in silence the bed
　Where angels would stoop to be blest.
Ye beautiful, heav'nly churchyard flowers,
Contrasted by weeds of lesser powers,
Smiling forth His power Divine,
Awaiting the Spring of ministering Time
Of quick'ning glory to shine
In the eternal light and love
Of the Holy One above.

May 26th, 1863.

ON THE REOPENING OF ALL SAINTS CHURCH,

CANTERBURY.*

May the smiles
Of Heaven's bright gleaming light be on this church,
Of renovated beauty, which to-day
Has been re-opened.　O for thanks and praise

* Those who remember what this church was when the restoration was commenced will be able to appreciate the success which has attended the efforts to remodel the interior. The pulpit, which has been made by Mr. Wiltsher, is one of the most artistic in the neighbourhood, and the new work may be favourably compared with any of the most recent ecclesiastical restorations.

In true benevolent spirit, rich and poor,
Thanking God—the object of their lives.
The end of which the hope of bringing home
To Him the outcast poor wanderer,
To that " eternal home " of rest and peace.
   Can we forget this day's imposing scene,
The holy mysteries of His strengthening power ?
The helping hand of unity and love,
This meeting, ah ! of unostentatious grandeur,
Of voluntary blessings and good will ?
The care and zeal of men whose earnest minds
Are fixed for doing good in praises of
Their heavenly Father, O most mighty God,
In light and joy of His all-smiling power
Of immortality !
              In His presence,
Yea, in the paths of mercy, truth, and light,
The pleasures of man's unrestrained joys,
Of earnest worship in the house of God,
Is known but to himself and to his Maker,
Devoted in the prayer of faith and hope
Of life eternal, joys which are to come
When Time, alas ! shall be no more.

HOPE FOR THE FUTURE.

As the shadows of night disappeared with the dawn,
   So the sorrows of mind passed away;
But let me not dwell on the past that is gone,
   But the coming of some future day.
Oh, rapturous thought of gentle sweet love,
   In grace but too virtuous to live;
In holiness here, but in glory above,
   In life-giving joy to arrive
To full glowing pow'r of Heaven's delight,
   Created for life-joy above.
How can I forget, tho' time's pass'd away?
   For the object of love will control:
Hope fills ev'ry passion, and conscience will say
The mind and the heart and the soul must obey
Her dictates to watch for some future day;
To meet such a loved one in triumph above,
In the realm of eternal joy-living love.

BIRDS' AND INSECTS' HOLIDAY.

Welcome, March,
Beauteous month of vocal lay,
What a glorious favoured day!
Birds and insects on the wing,
Hark! the musing Graces sing.
Soaring high in heav'nly fire,
Listen, yea, behold, admire,

The little songsters of delight—
Insects, birds, in clouded light.
Behold the tiny ants, how gay ;
Tens of thousands find their way
From beneath to work and play ;
The spider and the honey-bee
Mark their blissful poetry ;
Hark the cricket, listen, see !
E'en the grasshopper of merit,
Claiming to be their king-poet :
Full of life, the humble fly,
Cheering them that sing to die.
Worms and idle slugs, how long
Will ye listen to his song ?
All in Nature to befriend.
Hurly-burly to the end.
But before the day of Spring
Noisy insects should not sing :
And, of course, we give our reason-
'Cause such things are out of season.
Pass on, March, and quickly bring
The festive day of opening Spring :
Then, and not before, there's merit
Found to crown the insect-poet.
All before is discord jest,
Human listeners, why detest
Such sweet hymns ? Again we pray
For the glorious ripening day.
Come, then, holy Spring, how long
Shall we wait for Nature's song ?

Bud in beauty fairly blown,
Then sweet Nature's light to own,
By her wisdom-glory shown.
March on, March, to bring fair Spring,
For the little larks begin
On the twenty-fifth to sing,
To glorify the opening day—
The birds' and insects' holiday.
Stars of light and sun, oh, say,
Will ye listen to their lay?
And smile where attraction lies—
The little songsters in the skies—
Where the musing Graces rise.

A FRAGMENT.

" The Earth is the Lord's," and the fulness thereof;
All things He hath made are His own.
He called forth man from the dust of the earth,
And to dust, alas! man shall return :
But by light of His glorious power He hath shown
Ev'ry star in his beauty, bright, holy, and fair.
In the smiles of His grace, full of heavenly praise,
Congenial with reason, man's light is his prayer;
For by faith in the prayer of truth he obeys,
(As the Saints now of God in glory appear),
Advancing in holiness year after year,
Securing his heavenly wealth he holds dear,
Whilst he travels in smiles to the grave.

NATURE'S GIFTS.

Beauteous April, smiling in delight
To spread thy holy gifts upon the earth,
What new creations springing into life,
What delicacy, tenderness, what power,
What grace and beauty in the opening flowers !
In Nature's light come they forth but to teach
Men how to watch and find enjoyment here ;
By holy lessons of unsullied truth
To glorify the unseen hand of God
For His all-bounteous goodness, and to lead
Them to contemplate the happy passing hour
Of life and song in gratitude and praise,
Whilst man himself is passing to the grave
In full assurance of another life
Of unchanging glory.

April 1st, 1868.

JACK THE QUACK.

"Oh well we remember
The first of November,
A day of full trouble and woe,
From morning till night,
Poor Jack with no light
Could not steer the right way to go.

But Jack must be " right,"
For in a great fright
He clamber'd the pinnacle of fame,
To give public fun
By a glorious run
In the race to gain a good name.

A donkey so " blue,"
With changing green hue,
Is enough to attract any boor,
With burden so great,
Yet for his own sake
We'll give him the rein as before.

But now it is past
And the cobbler's last
Is fitting poor Jack a new shoe,
What's seen with our eyes
Indeed may surprise,
Though 'tis nothing to me or to you.

" Too much of one thing
Is good for nothing :"
So now we take leave of poor Jack ;
But should he still bray,
We'll give him more hay,
And do what we can for the quack.

Intellectual light
Of quackery and right
Should meet its reward by applause :
This tribute of right
In respect of its light
Must show its true meaning and cause.

Poor Jack's clouded face
Can never disgrace—
His impudence how can he know ?
We beg the poor knave
His charity save,
That the fruits of his labour may flow.

But just open your eyes
When the borrowed news flies,
For harmless indeed is poor Jack.
Let him do what he will,
By his glorious skill,
You'll remember he is but a quack.

THE SIEVES OF SOCIETY ;* OR, EVIL SLANDER.

Oh ! that malicious, petulant madness,
The fallacy of the unconscious mind,
Of petty senseless strife and cruel slander,
Revolting in the depth of sin and folly,

---

* " You would not pour precious wine into a sieve ; yet that were
as wise as to make a confidant of one of those 'leaky vessels' of
society that, like water-carts, seem to have been made for the express
purpose of letting out what they take in. There is this difference,
however, between the perforated puncheon and the leaky brain—the
former lays the dust, and the latter is pretty sure to raise one.
Beware of oozy-headed people, between whose ears and mouth there
is no partition. Before you make a bosom friend of any man, be
sure that he is secret-tight. The mischief that the non-retentives
do is infinite. In war they often mar the best-laid schemes, and
render futile the most profound strategy. In social life they sometimes set whole communities by the ears, frequently break up

Of emulating drunkenness.   Oh ! alas,
The serpent-tribe of circulating pow'r,
That ostentatious hissing—mortal dread !
What awful chills—for by the deadly sting
The soul becomes alarmingly afraid
At every symptom its excitement brings.
The spider-monkey chatters but to please,
Like a tailless scorpion does no harm,
Until a cure, a perfect cure, is made ;
For Busybody's inconsistent light
Only reflects the length of his long ears,
And by his own great shadow takes affright,
And so becomes more patient, self-controlled.
      But Nature's nature, alas !
A goose cannot be blamed for being one,
Nor can an ass be censured for stupidity ;
A rose cannot change its own insincerity,
Nor claim admiration from more lasting flowers.
The tittle-tattle of the busy tongue,
Or empty silence of the cunning knave,

families, and are the cause of innumerable misfortunes, miseries, and crimes.   In business they spoil many a promising speculation, and involve hundreds in bankruptcy and ruin.   Therefore be very careful to whom you intrust information of vital importance to your own interests, or to the interests of those you hold dear.   Every man has a natural inclination to communicate what he knows, and if he does not do so it is because his reason and judgment are strong enough to control this inherent propensity.   When you find a friend who can exercise absolute power over the communicative instinct—if we may so term it—wear him in your heart, ' yea, in your heart of hearts.'   If you have no such friend, keep your own counsel."

Only show the folly of their wisdom
In this embarrassed meritorious age—
Of small talk !
        But, alas ! that sensation,
That o'erpowering bliss of simple ignorance
Which marks the showman's constitutional vice,
Whilst banished by the pow'r of his freedom
From good society to repent alone,
In irritative folly and discredit.
Then Busybody, put up thy black flag
Of envy, hatred, malice, and revenge ;
Rather live to bless than persecute
The sorrowing soul—for where's the human bliss
Of iniquitous murder in the curse ?
   Remember, oh, alas ! remember,
The little time that's given man to live ;
To gain new life in light of holy truth
And grace Divine in the living God
Is short indeed.

WEARY DAYS.

" My life is full of weary days,
   But good things have not kept aloof,
Nor wandered into other days :
   I have not lacked thy mild reproof,
Nor golden largess of thy praise.

" And now shake hands across the brink
   Of that deep grave to which I go ;
Shake hands once more : I cannot sink
   So far—far down, but I shall know
Thy voice, and answer from below."

TENNYSON.

I would not o'er the brink shake hands,
   For thy tight grasp, alas ! I know
Would not give way in pit-fall sands
   Until we'd both sunk down below.

Too late, alas ! thy mild reproof,
   I might then hear with sad surprise ;
Then let me rather keep aloof
   To stretch my hand that thou may'st rise.

THE VERGER AND HIS VICTIMS.

IRRESISTIBLY amusing 'tis to see
   The sly demure, as senseless as a clod,
Each pompous verger with his massive key
   Unlocks the pew to one who's silver shod,
   To make a profit in the house of God.
   Another leader with his magic rod,
On the look-out for the accustom'd fee,
   And then to his snug nook to sleep and nod.

To dream perchance he's gain'd much by his wits.
　　There the poor, neglected, uncared-for stands
To reflect or look about till half in fits ;
　　No paltry bribe to slip into their hands ;
For what cares he ?—no matter where he sits ;
　　Bound to obey the strange law—for 'tis man's
　　Ambition to make profit of their lands,
Or churches where the public worship free
To make a profit by a ruinous fee—
Such is the glory of the insane blind,
Who seek below for what they never find.
　　We step aside to see the wiser pass,
　　For without cash the empty pews, alas !
Would ne'er get filled.　Go there 'twould be a crime
To fill the space where brighter stars should shine :
Let him who would deny the truth appear,
　　The man of straw confront to say I'm wrong.
'Tis for reform I write, no more I fear,
　　Nor do I care who would condemn my song ;
Were I but a philosopher, as wise
　　As bishops, deans, or priests who preach of love,
I'd give the vergers salve to anoint their eyes
　　To see themselves in the lowest place above,
Down among the dead men's bones they rise.
　　But all are equal in the house of God,
　　The thread-worn coat, ah ! ah ! and silver shod
Brought to the level at last—how odd,
　　To rot and feed the worms beneath the sod !
Then why, alas ! should " jingling cash " be given
　　To crown the joy of one who is so-so ?

'Twill never gain the highest place in Heaven,
   For vanity is what man seeks to know
   In that refined hypocrisy of show;
   To find the grandest place here below,
See yon cathedral, there the rich and poor
Separate (to " pray ") as they enter at the door.

THE CUP OF SORROW.

           MAN takes
His "drops" from the poison-cup of sorrow,
And thus degrades his spark of mental power,
By inebriate joy of stupefying
Madness.   Folly-wise errors to commit.
How like the bee that sips the venom sweet
From the beauteous maiden starlike flower,
Which smiles upon the unpretending haulm
Of a diseased potato.

MAN.

     CONDEMNED to perish !
Or was man born to find a higher place
   In that blest heav'nly mansion, there to see
The dreadful glory of His face,
In holiness of never-ending grace,
   The light and truth of all eternity ?

But what is man, that he should hope in death
  To live again in cloudless light above
With Him who giveth life-eternal breath
  In endless joy of holiness and love ?

" FLOWERS OF SULPHUR."

MYSTERIOUS SYMPATHY FOR SMALL THINGS.

          We strain the eye
At microscopic objects to discern
  Something for our good ; it is man's lot
To magnify small things, and then to learn
  To have compassion.

          Oh then sprinkle not
Flowers of Sulphur just to kill
  The unseen grubs, that strive to rise
Out from the earth to show their skill,
  Alas ! to tickle, to surprise :
  To buzz about 'mongst rich-dress'd flies,
Just to annoy, and make us ill,
  Or force a smile against our will,
  Are things most men despise.

Flowers of Sulphur, horrid drug !
  What must it be for those who keep it,
  And " recommend " their friends to eat it ?
  What makes man shudder ?   Ha ! one finds
A warning lesson (to the grub),

To little men that have great minds,
Who think they've powers to give a rub
In vulgar, simple, childish rhymes.

But Flowers of Sulphur, will it kill
    The "pent-up forces" of the nation?
Let that great chemist, if he will,
    Show forth his powers of education,
And thus prevent a child of skill
    From taking life of new creation.
The noxious creeping things of May
In Adam's blooming garland gay.

Well, Flowers of Sulphur he would lack
To kill the bug and save the quack,
Its singular properties might cheat.
    Then let us learn from "Nature's teaching."
Ask that wise man in Burgate Street,
    If he would have another greeting,
To give his friend another treat
(In something fresh that he could eat),
But keep his temper whilst he's preaching.
    To one who could no malice bear
    (God forbid, we all have care),
    Search the heart. it is not there.

Q

NAPOLEON.

SAD FATE.

SUCH is life :
One day in joyful prime upon the throne,
Another day forsaken and alone ;
 Those upon whom he honours showered,
 Gave wealth, distinction—ay, a monarch's power—
Exulting o'er the downfall of his dynasty, his throne.
 Does Fate decide so ill ? or will the prince
 Arise—a phœnix—if but to make these cowards wince ?

September 19*th*, 1870.

FEAR NOT THE EVIL SPEAKER.

HEED not,
 Nor fear the evil-speaker in disguise ;
 But shame the knave by registering his lies.
 The smallest spark of truth can never fade ;
 'Twill throw a light upon th' unguarded knave,
 And strip of " honour " him who would degrade
 The innocent ; forgetting God hath made
 Him not for secret guilt for which he toils.
  The designated liar may supply
  His cruel " items " even whilst he smiles
   To injure one (alas ! the tear and sigh),
   Unconscious, oh ! that God is ever nigh.
   Such knaves may seek for death, yet cannot die.

To meet the danger would they not retreat?
How can they face their God of truth and love?
Well may they tremble at the judgment-seat:
Each guilty conscience must his own case prove,
His dreaded thought of meeting Him above.

September 16*th*, 1870.

HARSH WORDS.

ANGRY words are not forgot
By him whose heart is broken;
Years may have passed, the hour and spot
Repeat themselves, for are they not
Remembered as just spoken?

September 16*th*, 1870.

"PAUL PRY."

"Two of a trade can ne'er agree."

PAUL PRY,
Or any other villain-spy
That would with artful means find full employ,
Must always be a simple-looking boy;
But not too simple, wanting other aid,
To run the risk of being mark'd, betrayed,
By those who disagree to get the trade.
The keener knave, or else the skilful jade

Will sure to get the better of her foes,
To make a mark where'er she pokes her nose.
To get the prize for artfulness indeed
A drowsy-honest look will sure succeed.

September 15th, 1870.

THE PLOUGHMAN'S CONFESSION.

DELICATE SUBJECT.

3 o'clock, A.M.

" WHEN I 'as done my morning's work,
    I'se ready for my ' mutton-chops ;'
A quart o' milk, a pound o' pork.
    But when I'se thirsty other slops ;
    The juice o' barleycorn an' hops.
'Tis then I cannot mind my stops,
    An' quite forgets about the crops,
    And that is how I gets the ' swops.' " *

September 15th, 1870.

DANCING BEARS.

THE mountebanks
Cut wondrous capers to amuse
    The poor barefooted swine of meaner station—
But what's so horrid as the creaking shoes
    Of those who dance to show their education ?

* To " swop " means to discharge.

SELF-PARTIALITY.

FRAGMENT.

SELF-OPINIONED
" Poets" and painters all must live
If they would rise to fame,
To sing and daub, to take and give,
And labour on in vain—
To die without a name.

September 9th, 1870.

FAITHFULNESS.

" Be thou faithful unto death, and I will give thee a crown of life."

" PERISH wealth, and power, and pride,
Mortal gifts by mortals given ;
But let faithfulness abide—
Faithfulness, the gift of Heaven."
Proves the lesson each must learn ;
For neither wealth nor education
Giveth such rewards in turn
As character and reputation
For faithfulness by truth upborne.

September 17th, 1870.

FALSE FRIENDS.

FALSE friends, alas ! will have no care
    For those in joy or sorrow ;
With chilling breath they wing despair,
    To horrify the morrow,
And blast the hope of all around
Wherein their " charities " abound.

September 11th, 1870.

LINES.

In affectionate remembrance of dear little Frank Elgar, who fell
asleep in the arms of Jesus, on the 15th of ninth month, 1870.

THANKS be to God
For giving that dear child His grace
    To live in Him ; then why
At his departure friends should weep
Because he closed his eyes in sleep
    And did not fear to die ?
    Then why that tear-drop in the eye ?
    Dear friends, weep not, alas ! nor sigh,
For now he lives with Him above,
In holiness of light and love—
    A star beyond the sky,
Smiling in the joy that's given,
To await his friends in Heaven.
    Are *we* prepared to die ?

September 19th, 1870.

ONE FOOL CAN ALWAYS SEE ANOTHER.

THE wisely foolish disagree
    About th' opinion of each other,
Or some good point he cannot see
    In his malignant silly bother.
Thus ignorant men are often heard
    To underrate a wiser brother,
By just three words that's most absurd,
    In answer to—" And you're another."

DECEIT.

THE faithless friend must have two hearts,
    An extra skin to shake off;
But then his double light imparts
    A power to force the mask off,
And bring to view that monkey-face,
    All grinning rage and pale,
Just to confirm his sad disgrace
    In having lost his tail.

SELF-DEVOTED PRAYER.*

LIKE helpless infants,
Great kings may only live to pine and fret,
Whilst fearing others (his) own sins forget ;
Born to trouble, every one has care,
· Yet all are equal if with kings we share
Our sympathy for self-devoted prayer :
For rich and poor have troubles to compare,
Humbled by the little knowledge given ;
 On earth a beggar, yet a crown to own ;
 Puff'd up with silly pride it may be shown
 On earth a king, but oh, in Heav'n unknown.

———◆———

THE BRIBER.†

Now "coals" are cheap,
The hireling that must claim our rightful notice
Is that bright object in his fustian suit ;
With well-feign'd virtue he can show what life is :

* A prayer composed by George the Third on the day of his coronation, found by one of the princesses in his desk :—"Keep me, O Lord, from silly and unguarded friends, and from secret enemies, and give me those things that are best for me, through Jesus Christ our Lord."
   † See Blue Book.

But to aspire
To something higher,
To sink below the level of the brute—
Cold, forsaken'd, and without a fire,
To wallow and to perish in the mire.

A COMPLAINT.

Alas ! how many are starved in this land of plenty, flowing with milk and honey.

LONGING for food in this day of confusion,
How many half-starved are denied absolution,
  Whilst the wise men of straw meet to feed !
But then these great feasters have not a bad notion
To angle but for the gold-fish of the ocean,
  Whilst the dinner-bell announces their creed,
To show these divines are so full of devotion—
  They forget the poor standing in need.

SPECULATION.

SOME speculate to lose a fortune,
  Some by chance-luck only gain
Nothing but rude jeers and scoffing,
  Perhaps to drive each one insane,
  When his efforts are in vain.

September 15th, 1870.

A WOMAN OF RENOWN.

OH, charming woman ! lovely sight !
Reeking, wagging, day and night,
With knotted hair in such a plight,
And two black eyes not very bright,
Having almost lost her sight,
Reeling forward left and right—
 All modesty destroy'd,
 For luxury enjoyed :
  The elevation of the head
   With that blue tiny bonnet,
   Well-trimm'd of course with green and red,
   And yellow bows upon it.
But how delightful does she look
 Whene'er she would beguile us !
Poor charming swell !   But, hark, that rook
 In angry tones upbraid us
For looking after one so grand—
 A beauty without paint ;
But who would take her thick brown hand
 Unless she were to faint ?
  More charming creature couldn't be,
  Her goggle eyes to turn on thee ;
 Her looks would make one shake,
  Her winding tongue—but, hark ; oh ! see —
 Where is that hissing snake ?

September 14th, 1870.

THE DRUNKARD'S SOLILOQUY.

OH, change my taste, ye mighty gods,
    That I no more may be
An interesting man of "odds,"
    But from all troubles free,
Such as swimming in the head,
Oh, raise me now (that I am dead),
    To find new life in *tea !*

A SCOLDING WIFE.

BETTER were she dumb :
The loved, impoverished, scolding wife,
    Sweet vocal music charms,
The highest note must give new life,
Should one be lucky in the strife
        To fall into her arms,
            To make the poor man glum.

DIFFERENT GRADES OF DIRTY SWELLS.

            WHY should we scorn,
Or satirize those dirty men of sense,
    Who overrate themselves but to bewitch
The wiser who can scarcely count their pence,
    Nor change their linen when they've got the itch ?

Another class, dressed up just to amuse,
    Still wiser urchins, that hold consultation
About the cost of worn-out coats and shoes,
    Given them by men of every station
      To polish off, and show their "eddecation."
There is of course another class of swells;
    The downright fop to greater taste aspires,
That's so polite to nod to all the gals,
    And take advantage if one only smiles:
Some do suppress, some titter, some laugh out;
    For who can help it when these "gents" of show
Parade the streets with belles who strut about
To talk of mighty things? We hear them shout,
    " How art thee, dear," politely bowing low.
Then for a gossip, but in sense obscure;
The pavement taken up—perhaps no fewer
Than eight or ten of these fine swells of choice,
Each showing which has got the loudest voice;
Making free with names of those who're passing,
    Perhaps in obscene language just to teach
A lesson to the boys who sweep the crossing,
    To check them in their work that they may reach
To something that may end in issue frightful—
A Grub-street swell;—but there 'tis all delightful
    To each poor dear neglected little urchin,
    Where sickening sports are seen behind the curtain.

September 15th, 1870.

TO A SECRET ENEMY.

GIVE me a heart that I may pray
For those who'd injure me ;
Yet let each unkind creature know
I have no hope for thee.

September 14th, 1870.

REFLECTIONS ON A LITTLE COUNTRY CHURCH.

YE of th' adjoining parish
Behold the church (ay, more ! go, hear the preacher) ;
Both lame and blind, have strength that ye may reach her,
To learn a lesson from a godly teacher,
Who bids us watch to keep the Sabbath holy,
But to His glory.

September, 1870.

"CIVILIZATION."*

" RELIGION and industry " find the keys
To open unto us the heavy gates
To life and liberty and sweet success,
To give us joy and peace for evermore.

September 14th, 1870.

---

* " Religious Life in England."

FOREIGN NEWS.

INSENSIBILITY.

                    OH, sick'ning news !
Why tell us that poor Jack wants oats,
Or of those horrid "things" in coats,
    Which say their grace and pray,
And then to cut each other's throats,
    And crumble into clay ?

September 16th, 1870.

"GREAT MEN."

GREAT men have often little minds,
    They're selfish in their praise ;
Their charity's of sacred source—
Their pride and blindness is a curse.

On barren land their double-face
        Might rise a trifle higher—
        Nay, set the Thames on fire !
But till the water's in a blaze
They'll get no universal praise.

HYPOCRITES.

Some labour only in deceit
To earn the bread they cannot eat,
To get in debt, but never pay—
They care not what they do or say,
Yet make long faces when they pray,
Whilst scheming for another day :
They cringe and fawn to be thought good—
Such characters are understood :
They live on flattery—false praise !
Until they get lost in the maze ;—
Puff'd up (despised), so many ways
Spending their idle fruitless days.

June 19th, 1867.

SABBATH TEACHERS.

Parent of immortal love
   Of wisdom, power, and light,
   Before the coming night
Oh, smile Thy wisdom from above,
   In holiness delight,
Upon the teachers of Thy truth,
Who lead the innocent in youth
To serve Thee and do Thy will,
That holy mission to fulfil,

And prayerfully atone
(At Thine eternal throne)
For ev'ry sinful word and thought
Displeasing to that One who bought
Our precious souls to save.

PLUCK'D TO DIE.

WHY pluck that little flower?
It was a little beauty-queen,
Peeping modestly unseen
From beneath its bright green leaves,
Full of smiling power.
Little gem of virgin-beauty,
Glowing in the light of duty,
Pluck'd to die : oh! sad regret,
Care bereft, who can forget?
Little gem of light Divine,
Thou shalt live—yea, smile and shine,
To bloom in Paradise again,
To glorify His holy name,
In the power of sacred truth,
To smile forth eternal youth.

A CHILD'S PRAYER.

O FATHER, give me that glorious food
Which rectifies and purifies the heart,
That the Holy Spirit may dwell in me,
And make me a happy child of Heaven,
For the sake of our blessed Redeemer,
Thy dear Son, Jesus Christ our Lord.   *Amen.*

WHAT'S IN A NAME?

WHAT! shall we " learn how not to do?"
    Is not omission full of grief?
Yet what is that to me or you,
    If bold addition's no relief?
Just take the letter " o " from good,
    And add the " d " to evil,
And thus we see our loving God,
    And hateful foe the devil.
And so in ev'ry mighty name
There's good or evil in the same,
But how the noisy title fell
This anagram will partly tell :—
We find a nameless note in stone,
    And thus in sporting time,
We make the mite, but then we own,
    There's nothing left to rhyme.
Ah! here's omission then the quack to please,
We sift our coals that they may rhyme with cheese,

R

And thus the cure is made in plaintive tone,
Whilst melancholy sighs a savage groan
Of hateful power which can ne'er deceive
The simpleton, if he would believe,
There's nothing in the taking of a name,
It is the changing title gives the pain.
Thrust a greatness on a thinking fop,
And he will soon be on the mountain top,
There to fan himself with ruffles bright,
In " mity " glory, and of course delight.
The world would bow obedience to his claim,
And pay the highest tribute to his name ;
The " mity " object magnified by care,
For worthless homage which is not so rare,
But here the rhyming beauty is unknown,
Revealing fruit before the seed is sown.

THE GLORIOUS STARS ABOVE.

Look up, behold
Th' unfading beauty of the stars,
　　Their vivid colours bright ;
Smiling to give Him praise,
　　And cheer the night with light.
Encircled round th' heavenly gate,
　　His glory to impart ;
Shining, ay, to show the way
　　To God when souls depart.

Divinely beautiful they shine,
  Ten thousand worlds above,
Where disembodied spirits roam,
  Perchance in holy love.
But who can tell the glorious sight
  The spirit-eye shall see,
Beyond the stars so heav'nly bright,
  In life eternity?
We have faint glories to delight
  On earth, the " star-like " flower ;
But soon, alas ! like man, is gone
  Its beauteous life and power.
Then let us contemplate in praise
  The glorious stars above,
And learn by faith that He will raise
  All men to light and love.
Ungrateful man ! what is his life ?
  Hath he an hour to spare ?
Why should he live for cruel strife,
  If he new joys would share ?
Why should he think because he's blest
  With riches God hath given,
Or that because he's better dress'd
  'Twill carry him to Heaven ?
It matters not to God, the heart
  That seeks his Maker's trust ;
E'en rich and poor must soon depart,
  They are alike but dust.

January 31st, 1865.

BUDS OF SPRING.

LOVELY buds of Heaven-bright beauty,
　　Full of living hope ye are ;
Full of Heaven-inspired duty ;
　　Full of wisdom's light and power :
Full of animating joy—
Perfect bliss without alloy.

Infant children newly given,
　　Emblems of sweet buds of bliss,
Blooming for eternal Heaven,
　　Little tempting flowers to kiss :
Young and tender, full of joy—
Perfect bliss without alloy.

Little children now to duty,
　　Lisp your little prayer to God :
" Our Father, Lord of Heaven,
　　Guide us with Thy staff and rod :"
Night is come, O seek for joy—
Perfect bliss without alloy.

THE SABBATH CALL.

MAN is spiritually summoned to serve his God in the
　　living Church
In solemn prayer on the sacred day of appointed holy
　　rest,
To adore his Maker earnestly in that Heaven-tuned song

Which gives peaceful conscience—breathing love for all
    men :
There he collects wisdom's precious highest gifts—
That heavenly living exhaustless material
By which the new-born soul is formed for eternity :
That he, steadfast in faith, become a living majestic pillar
To support that canopy of heavenly glorious light
Which reflects the unchanged beauty of the immortal
    pictures
Of angel-innocence, purity, honesty, virtue, truth, charity,
    and love—
That grace memory's eternal consecrated walls
Of the house of prayer—the living Church of God ;
Of which Christ is the foundation of spiritual strength.
To the darkest shades, where troubled mortals are,
God's spiritual warning with His mercy comes,
For light—ah ! glorious light, is everywhere—His living
    Church,
Bidding man before the dawn of day
Obey His call, ere it be too late ;
But alas ! the time man has to live is short indeed.
And if he's blind to spiritual law, how can he find
The sacred key which unlocks the gate of the narrow
    road
Which leads the nearest way to Paradise ?

SCANDAL.

OH, cruel spirit of savage delight,
Send forth thy raging flame, smoke, and lava
To the full extent of thy boundary,
So that thy triumphant shame in glory
May be the warning of thy consequence.
       Ah ! spirit of darkness,
Thy nature is for slaughter and to wound;
And tens of thousands fall to thy delight,
Till thine own fire shall have consumed itself.
Thy erring blindness,—self-deceiving power,
Thy wretched revenge can ne'er touch the soul,
Nor can thy royal name be heard in Heaven.

LANGUAGE OF CASH.

       By its tinkle,
Cash speaketh all languages known to the world :
   Should the rich (of stentorian lungs)
Become poor, then their speech, by adversity change,
   Might as well have been born without tongues.

Cash teacheth more languages known than all schools :
   So coveted, loved, for its charms ;
It will put clever heads on the shoulders of fools,
   Give the ignorant poor its royal arms.

The mountebank-puffs and quacks may display
    Ready wit, wisdom, learning, absurd ;
By cash the very deaf can hear what they say,
    But without, they seldom are heard.

QUEEN'S ENGLISH.

In " darkness,"
  The pedant who violates the rule
    Of grammar must be right ;
    If ignorance makes him bright,
Why then false English makes the fool
  Look *wiser* without light.

September 7th, 1870.

MY STARS ! MY STARS !

      Ye comet-like
Close shaving critics, why oppose the strong
  Immortal gods so full of princely zeal,
(In melting love) for doing what is wrong?
  Such envied merit only can reveal
The secret malice of a wicked thing,
  In finding fault with Peter Spoiler's song.

December 12th, 1866.

AN INSECT'S REVENGE.

HARK, the "death-watch :"—a spider's tick,
Calling for its mate to aid the sick—
The tame and foolish flies who come to see
The spider's feast of life and liberty,
Who welcomes in with dignified grace
To join the dead that lie about the place.
Hark, hark ! that buzz : another fly in fix --
The mischief making spider's cunning tricks
Have overcome the genius of the fly—
Entrapped, now kicking, gracefully to die.
A powerful wasp now comes to gaze in doubt,
And would the fly relieve, the spider rout,
But being half afraid, he could not strike
A deadly blow, yet murder he would like
To thus commit, but having lost his sting,
He could not see what honour it would bring :
" Shall I revenge ?" yet to himself would say,
" Why should the flies come in the spider's way ?"
An industrious bee comes forward with a bound,
And flings the stingless wasp upon the ground ;
Their close contention the spider soon espies :
That simple envy brings him new supplies.
But such is life : ambitious power and station,
Yea, over-educated men of ev'ry nation
Often show their want of education.

THE DEPARTED CHRISTIAN.

UNFETTERED by the living light of God,
Yet bound by chains of eternal love,
Applauded by innocent, smiling truth,
And crown'd in happiness by angel faith,
Which glorious Time had watched to secure
In silent memory for the faithful.

QUEEN MAY.

BRIGHT queenly May of life—enchanting song,
The brightest stars of heaven show forth their light
To crown thee—ah ! what evidence of truth—
The fragrant blossoms of admiring grandeur,
But alas ! so soon to fade and die.
  Now in thy youth the sublime
Encircling glory of thy spotless gems,
So cheering to the eye of the beholder ;
That Nature's so enraptured with the sight,
She glorifies thy gifts in songs of praise :
But, who can understand the secret joy ?—
The woodland flowers smiling in delight,
And blooming weeds of ev'ry shade and colour,
Pure and holy in their graceful robes
Of sunlight beauty.
  But, mark the glorious change, how many stars
Are fixed, but for a time to show His power
In living light, as perfect works of God.
May 1st, 1868.

JANUARY AND THE PASSING MONTHS.

BLEST January!
We welcome thee, O happy month, in praise
Of life and beauty, of thy few short days.
Thy life, tho' short, is full of living grace,
And soon in death thou'lt find a resting place;
A few short days and February's light
Will then relieve to give thee rest, delight;
For in thy death e'en Nature will rejoice
To welcome in, O happy cheering voice
Of February, rising power to give
New life and beauty a little while to live.
And then comes March hast'ning on in Spring
To heavenly joy, new glories yet to bring—
Comes glowing Summer smiling without grief,
Whilst Winter's watching, here to give relief;
For so the days and months and years pass on,
And in their time Death comes and we are gone.
When Time and Nature shall have pass'd and gone,
And out of sleep awakes the coming morn—
Man soon shall see his God of Light Divine.
Can he not see Him now in faith sublime?
Look up and serve Him, O the God of Heaven,
In holiness of new-born light that's given;
For all His works the good works man hath done
A sure reward: we pray His Kingdom come!
We pray for all, that all may reign with Him
Our Maker, God, our Father, Heav'nly King.

Blest January, happy month of light,
We glory in thy sacred gifts delight,
And as in morn may'st thou find joy in night
In holy sleep, in glory ever bright!

A LETTER FROM CANTERBURY TO A FRIEND AT DOVER.

DEAR FRIEND,

   I SHOULD have written you long before
Had I have been a member of your corps:
A little practice—oft my gun I take,—
Indeed you know I never do mistake!
A *dozen foes to owe!*—I might retire—
Yet when I see a chance I always fire:
But then, of course, I make my game select,
And never fire but when it takes effect.
I sometimes angle—when with fish beset,
But when they get entangled in my net
I never bait with gnat or fancy fly—
The artful fish, of course, would ne'er come nigh!
The other day, I had a fancy feel
To feed a shark upon a slippery eel.
How strange, indeed, these fish are sometimes green,
Though always blue when in low-water seen!
There always was, and always will be fun,
For in the season dogs will have their run:

But out of season sometimes you will spy
A troubled imp—but he is sure to die ;
For as I've said before, I take sure aim,
My point is gain'd if once I see the game.
It is the sport, ah, yes, the fun I crave ;
My just ambition is my " cakes " to save.
But now, I think, I've nothing more to write,
'Tis not the " cakes and ale " which give delight,
It is the triumph over wrong in right ;
I'll charge my gun whenever may be found
Bears and bulls, or foxes on my ground ;
But as to insects just a touch will show—
A little twig—I'll tell you what to do—
And yet I think the act is cruel too ;
Your Dover friends might say you had no pity,
But then a town is so unlike a city.
But stop—another time I'll tell you all ;
I may perhaps find means to give a call ;
'Tis nigh post-time, indeed I fear 'tis past ;
I'll promise you this shall not be my last.

THE FOPLING.

CONSIDER well the homage due
    To every foppish fool,
And give him credit for the few
    Small " changes " got at school.

Such emptiness, how plain to view!
  So full of vain delight—
A graceful "ornament," 'tis true.
  A diamond without light.

An ignorant, silly fop, we know,
  Can without science rise
To castles in the air, and show
  His plumage in the skies.

Animated by his dreams
  Of folly, 'tis a rule
Not to listen to his screams,
  Nor send him back to school.

A FRAGMENT.

  "'Tis noble only to be good ;
Kind hearts are more than coronets ;" the smiles
And kindnesses in little things secure
Love—insidious power—to elevate
The soul to Heaven.

  Man's life, tho' brief on earth,
Is full of hope, the good inspired by God,
Love that changeth not in mundane life
Nor's found deceitful : never changing love,
Faithful in the light of God above,
  Marked out and crowned for heavenly glory.

November 10th, 1864.

SUCH IS LIFE.

LIFE, how like a candle lit up, doom'd
     To give but little light in flecting time ;
'To dwindle down the lasting snuff consum'd—
               Death to find.
Mysterious is His wondrous dispensation,
     Pass'd by Death to immortality ;
For ev'ry death is life of new creation—
               Such is life.

MAN'S PILGRIMAGE TO HEAVEN.

MAN looks up in prayer and blesses God ;
He views the twinkling stars of living light—
The glorious sun and moon in smiling beauty :—
Animated by these holy truths,
Overwhelmed with thoughts of heav'nly life,
He travels on in glorious sweet delight
To his eternal home.
               He beholds his God,
As he contemplates His love and wisdom,
Remembering as he does man's but dust ;
Yet by his holy change of living joy,
He pursues his way to Heaven in earnest,   .
Blissful hope of his salvation.

TRUTH.

E'EN as a little child,
In light of virtue like the infant give
  That holy proof of purity and love,
Such wisdom-grace of innocence to live
  In confidence of smiling truth above ;
To bid the world—deceitful world—adieu,
For power of truth creates the heart anew ;
  In light of joy to give eternal breath ;
Yea ! truth alone will bring bright Heaven to view,
  And give real life beyond the shades of death.

"ABANDON SIN."

ABANDON sin and enter in
  The presence of His Light
Of holy love which smiles above,
  Reviving pow'r delight.
Learn to pray—ah ! thus prepare,
For faith and truth can enter there :
" Come," He saith, " O man, yea come—
Come ye sinful every one."
    Abandon sin
      For holy pleasure—
    Ha ! glory in
      His heavenly treasure
      Of glory without measure.

Sing His song of holy love,
Prepare to meet thy God above :
　 O ! then Death shall bring thee light
　 　 And glory pow'r,
　 　 In that hour
　 　 Thy soul shall take her flight
　 To that mysterious world above
Of heav'nly joy and godly love.

WISDOM'S LIGHT AND TRUTH.

　 　 O WISDOM of light !
How blest indeed are all thy holy truths,
Sweet corresponding beauties in Nature,
Smiling (under His eternal care)
Admiration's inexpressive praise,
To the great Almighty Giver of Life,
So teaching man how he should live to God,
To gain that boundless joy of living light
Which smiles above.
　 　 　 　 O wisdom of truth !
Yea, that better choice of enlightened love
Which glorifies the faithful living soul
To heav'nly joy.   O that gladd'ning prospect
Of immortality—a life in God,
By wisdom's light and truth of holiness
In man, immortal man !

TRUE RELIGION.

TRUE religion makes man great,
   Noble, wise, and kind ;
Lifted to that highest state
   This humbled soul can find
Joys that truth and love create,
   In holiness of mind.
His destiny is fixed above,
   Where life's rewards are given,
And nought can mar the joys of love—
   The light and life of Heaven.

December 10*th*, 1868.

"GOOD FRUIT."

        WHO can say
The medlar's famous when he's " rot ?"
   Green gooseberries good when fine ?
Or cherries when they have large stones ?
   Or apples of thick rind ?
The pine or fir without its cones,
   Small grapes that would be mine—
   Such qualities, ay, of the vine ;
The hazel or the filbert lack
More praise, because the nut to crack
   Requires a power divine—
As toothless men oft cut and hack
To take what they cannot give back.

S

But whilst the orchards we survey
    We find our trees of state,
For young or old we search, I say,
    But seldom find the date.
For my part, I would let them grow
    To flourish, ay, and please ;
But when I find a tree "so-so,"
Giving too much fruit, you know,
    I'd cut him up at ease.
For what's the use of giving rubs
Among the aromatic shrubs
    E'en in their spicy breeze ?

PRAYER.

PRAYER alone can give relief,
    And raise the down-cast soul above ;
Those holier joys from changing grief
    Is given but in His smiles of love
To him who fondly clings to God.
    So thus improve the time that's given
In holiness to seek above
    New life of joy—the light of Heaven.

Prayer, ay ! earnest prayer can give
    That solid joy beyond the grave ;
Without it none can really live ;
    Who would neglect their soul to save ?

Prayer alone can find delight
In that last hour when death shall strike—
The happy soul shall take her flight
To everlasting light of light.

March 30th, 1867.

CHURCHYARD WEEDS.

THE smallest weed-like flower may bear
    A cheerful smile again,
Rank stinging-nettles—who would care
    To touch the churchyard weeds that share
Man's blasting scorn ?—will death then spare
    The flower without a name ?

October 16th, 1866.

HOPE.

    WHAT is man ?
Born to trouble and to suffer long, alas !
Nothing here to rest upon, but pass
On to the grave in hope to find
The well-spent life will bring peace in the end,
    And give to him that joy-eternal rest
In Heaven's delight, to meet his Saviour-friend,
    Glorified among the living blest ;
Where holiness of virtue lives to shine
In smiling truth of living light divine.

"LITTLE COCK ROBIN."

FULL sixty years Rob lived unrecognised,
  For sportive humour in all kinds of weather ;
We hear him twitter whilst he feeds on flies
Now generating from the dirty hides
  That's soon to be converted into leather.

THE PINE OR FIR TREE.

      THE inexperienced
May wound the tree whose heart's consigned
To do all honour ; who possess the mind
To bore or tap the graceful stately pine
For his " spruce-beer," his medicinal wine,
Pitch, resin, tar, and e'en turpentine ;
But mark his curious cones, delightful toys
To please small men and overgrown great boys.
  Touch not the produce of that fruitful fir,
  Whose pitch or tar will soil your finger, sir ;
  Yet bless—oh, bless that self-admiring pine,
    Dispensing liquids of eternal good,
  That pre-exist such properties divine—
    Not in the bark, but simply in the wood.

THE CORK TREE.

How many have become shipwreck'd and lost
By disregarding thee of little cost ;
Thy glorious bark, and not thy wood, can save
The inexperienced from untimely grave ;
And yet how many do anticipate
The living glory when it is too late !

THE TWO NOTIONS.

WISE NOTION.

There is one act that cures the envious man :
    If he who's wounded is still kind and civil,
To help the knave with " loaded good," he can
    Redeem the fool, and drive away the devil.

FOOLISH NOTION.

The polished fool may sometimes be caressed,
    Fed and courted simply through his life,
    To have his way whilst goaded on for strife,
    Like some unrivalled simpleton to know
(Because he may have money, be well-dressed,
    Minus of heart and mind, in boastful show),
    That there is none so grand as he below
To typify the virtue of the bless'd
Man ; understand the hint—then guess the rest ;
    The unforbidden knave could be no foe,
    If, like himself, mankind would be " so-so."

THE WAY TO GOD.

THE gifts of God—what love !
  He sends us all good things
    On wings
Of angel-light, to prove—
Our hardened hearts to move.

The love of God, what power
  Of holy joyous light,
    To right
And perfect ev'ry hour,
E'en the smallest flower !

The way to God is light,
  The Bible is His word :
    Good Lord,
Teach us truth delight—
The Holy Cross in sight.

But let us never miss
  The chance of pray'r and praise ;
    Few days
To gain eternal bliss
And heavenly happiness.

"FALLING STARS."

How gloriously sublime!
Behold the wonders of the sky,
But not with superstition's eye
    In this mysterious hour.
Oh! mark each star, behold the sight,
Ten thousand sparks of flaming light,
    Under His all-guiding power,
The "so-called shooting stars of fire,"
    Illuminating space around,
Falling, ay, to rise still higher,
    Whilst the world is upside down :—
Such a shower of stars sublime,
    To move in glory and proclaim
To every nation, every clime,
To attract the thoughtless, how divine!
    The teaching man to praise His name.

November 13th, 1866.

A GOOD NAME.

    Tho' man dies,
And his form of loveliness fades away,
Yet every sentiment of affection lives
In the heart of memory's joyous light.
The glorious smile of beauty is on him
Whilst his name of spiritual goodness
(Gained by godly virtue) is breathed in Heaven.
O, that sweet glowing, fondly trusting love,
That living holy light of new-born power,

Which coins the name and purifies the soul
In the diamond path of short-given life
Which leads to the grave—ah! to Paradise.
Tho' short-lived, and the trembling eyelids fall
In death, yet man's rightful name is blest
In the intimate delight of glory;—
Immortalised in every living joy
By the angel-saints of eternal God.

THOUGHTS ON DEATH.

What is man, with all the gifts of mind,
　Loaded with fruitful blessings to be blest?
Whilst 'neath that burden seeking but to find
　Pitying Nature's smile to give him rest?
But was he born to glorify the earth?
　Then, why in time so soon to pass away?
Why should his day so shorten from his birth,
　Be track'd by death to vanish in decay?

A CELTIC FABLE.

　　　　　Unloyal bees!
It shows superior judgment of the queen
　Only to crown great workers for her good;
　All idle monsters she turns out for food,
And bids her soldiers strike whene'er is seen

All lazy drones who live to suck her blood,
And rob her of her honey-wine in store :
Such royalty they court, we've said before.

So eager, yea, they will not wait their turn,
But go to rob, cut down, are seen no more ;
 Her palace gates are closed by growing ferns,
And many a hireling standing at the door,
 To 'watch with rage, the hungry spider learns,
How many dead lie scattered on the floor.
 Impatient for a feast, they teach their young
 To mark the living outcast to be hung,
Entangled in their webs they've nearly spun—
The queen comes out to glorify the fun.

The Fenians may take caution by their wrong,
 Altho', for gain, to Royalty they'd kneel ;
Their disloyal powers of course cannot last long :
 They twist and turn as slippery as an eel :
 Such small fry out of water now must feel
Themselves as dead to good government,
Or dying out of their true element.

A HOME ABOVE.

THERE is a home of light above,
 Where saints and angels dwell
In holiness of joyous love ;
 But who on earth can tell

The future blessing now in store
    For all who serve aright?
The holy saints who've gone before
To live upon that happy shore
    Are crown'd with pure delight.

There is indeed a home above,
    Where angel-saints of God
Have suffer'd on the cross for love,
    And in His footprints trod.
They've passed to find eternal rest
Among the holy living blest.
    Behold them—they are there!

December, 1866.

THE WINTER AND THE ROBIN.

WINTER's rejoicing in his pride;
But can his powers long last
Of nipping frost and cutting winds,
Whilst life is ebbing fast?
    The snow is falling, drifting by,
    Dark and low'ring is the sky,
    E'en song-birds cease to sing;
    But the sun is rising high,
    A sudden change to bring—
    For Winter soon must die.
But little Redbreast, tame and fair,
Now homeless, without food,
Starving, dying, full of care,
He finds no comfort in the wood,
Where all the trees are bare.

Open wide the casement door,
Let poor Robin roam ;
Agonized, distracted, poor,
Oh, offer him a home !

AMBITION WITHOUT LIGHT.

In glory of Nature,
Ye frogs of damp places, why croak in the dark ?
Whilst cobblers and thinkers profound
Would listen to honour, eulogize for a lark ;
Cruel boys, for vain sport, at low-water mark
Assemble, but to wound and confound.

Awake and rejoice in the sunlight of pleasure ;
Small stars have all vanish'd, begin ;
Pay homage to birds that have poetic treasure :
Caw, caw, hark the rooks ! see them all flock together—
Glorious in song such rhyme and such measure,
To prompt the small insects to sing.

Come, listen, ye bards, why sadden'd and weeping ?
Cheer up with the larks, sing, rejoice ;
Whilst the sweep your own chimneys is busily sweeping,
Why drown that discordant man's voice ?
Let him rise and sing chorus with the cawing rooks, but
His genius is far above all ;
In the light of ambition, tho' blacken'd with soot,
In glory of triumph to fall.

FALSE GUIDES.

FALSE teachers, heed not what they say,
　But look to God and live,
His holy light will show the way
　To power, and freedom give.

Is there not one true holy Church,
　Tho' many creeds are given ;
That gain of knowledge, man's research,
　To carry him to Heaven ?

Wheat and tares together grow,
　But to find fault with one—
To war against the good we know
　Would cause some dying fun.

There are good men, undoubtedly,
　Who for kind acts are blest,
But by their holy fruit we see
　They differ from the rest.

The kindly Shepherd knows His own,
　Would suffer none to stray ;
In smiling pity from the Throne
　He leads them safe away.

The little lambs of so much cost,
　Ha ! when the wolf comes nigh,
He guards them all that none be lost,
　That th' hungry foe may die.

But numerous are vain quacks of fame ;
   The black sheep who can know
   May well by science show,
Or try to count the drops of rain
   As to count the stars below—

Who hold their heads so very high,
   Their narrow minds misgiving.
But as the beam is in the eye
   They're counted dead whilst living.

May 22nd, 1867.

THE GOSPEL POWER.

      WITH humble bend,
In holy faith, man offers up his pray'r,
And so embraces e'en that spiritual light
Which operates upon the mind with pow'r,
To change the heart e'en to affecting love,
Which lives eternally Divine with God :
Thus man partakes the glory of His Church,
And so advances step by step, till he
Meets his Saviour in the realms above,
In blissful glorious eternity.
Happy effect the Gospel pow'r assigns
To ev'ry thinking man who treasures hope
In his Almighty ever-living God's
Eternal love and merciful care—
Glorious salvation.

PRIDE.

PITY the slave who seeks a name
For tinsel glory, pride and fame—
    Deny him not his will;
Of sorrow's dim disgraceful shades,
Of sinful darkness which invades
    His noble light and skill.

His ears so long may serve as wings,
And carry him to higher things—
    Why judge ye of his grace ?
Such vanity and pride below
    Deserve a better place.

Then let him rise to full employ,
To show the " greater lights " his joy—
    Alas ! but that's not all ;
For other fowls soon would rise,
Dispute his glory in the skies,
Peck at his ears, pick out his eyes,
    Despatch him in the fall.

" THE WICKED SHALL BE TURNED INTO HELL."

    OH, sorrow's dread !
Ever dying, yet never dead :
In mental pain to live again
    Under the distant ray ;
Midst Satan's legions ever to dwell
    After the Rising Day.

The wicked, false, corrupted heart
    Can feel no joy below,
Its endless gloom—ah ! bitter smart!
    Supplies eternal woe.

THE STARS OF HEAVEN.

YE glorious orbs of light-smiling beauty,
    Ye stars of enchanting spirit-giving love,
Ye seraphs and cherubs of heavenly duty,
    Lead us, O guide us, to glory above !
Ye messengers of light, redeeming the time,
    Smiling in silence of mystery deep,
How solemn and beautiful, holy, sublime !
    Let the heavenly glory awake us from sleep.
O ! shine forth His joy to await us in death,
Ye messengers of holy light-giving breath,
That we in one slumber awake in His light,
In the glorious realms of eternal delight.

FRAUD.

By studied falsehood man conceals his fraud,
Under the guise of friendship haunts a brother,
To give his tortured slave a restless mind —
E'en by help a false relief.

Oh, ruinous fraud!
With what dismay the victim finds his friend—
A sublime foe—himself a glorious fool ;
When he with trembling awe is o'erwhelmed
By cold adversity, cruelly taught
To learn of wisdom when it is too late !

———·———

FRIENDSHIP.

How dear are those true friends of mirth
Who live to watch us from our birth,
And strive to lift us from the earth
    In smiles of holy love !
Creating gladness, and to give
Their holy friendship whilst they live ;
    The inmost soul to move
By gentleness and loving mood,
Which in holiness record
    Good tidings from above.

November 19th, 1867.

———·———

SPRING.

I LOVE to ramble in the lofty woods,
    And contemplate the glory of His power,
To hear the song of Nature's life renew'd,
    'Mongst the verdant weeds and budding flower.

The primrose, violet, in the cooling shade,
  Refreshed in glory by the heav'nly dew,
By wisdom-power all for glory made,
  We're lost in wonder as they come in view.
So learn of Him, great God, as 'tis His will,
That we should trace His light, unerring skill,
And watch in praise, eternally to feed
Upon His giving glory.

        Spring is come!
O happy, joyous season of delight,
How in the light of mirthful song
And mysterious joy! cheering beauties
Spring up around in holy order,
In liberty of light and godly power!
Glorious are the honoured gifts of God:
The hills and valleys speak His living praise:
The fertile fields smiling in delight,
In wakeful glory of the tender bud;
The beauteous flowers, full of living grandeur,
Smiling truths of light and life-perfection,
Exulting in sweet Nature's living power
Of marvellous, joyous beauty.

    March 29th, 1864.

THE PERMANENCY OF NATURE.

      THOUGH man must die,
Yet Nature's full of holy living grandeur:
There is no blemish in her smiling beauty:

That quick'ning glory of immortal light
Smiles to change the doubting heart of man,
And teach him how to live and see aright
The way to Heaven.

His tender grace,
O matchless proof of wisdom, pow'r divine!
The changing seasons glow in watchful praise
Of Him : such confidence, trust, unerring light,
Shows reality of a Spirit—God,
Of tender mercy and undying love.

ADIEU, FEBRUARY! MARCH IS COME!

SHORT-LIVED February! of lovely innocence, alas! thou art gone!
We would that thou couldst have prolonged thy stay ;
Thy glorious deeds have given access to peace,
Thy sweet repose shall gain thee strength to reappear
To breathe forth Nature's future gifts divine,
And re-illume another opening year.
Thou wert foremost, constant in thy trust and duty,
Approaching only what could mark thy skill.
Farewell! blest happy month! how full of wisdom!
Thy departure gives new life to glowing March,
And lengthening days to multiply thy gifts.
The crocus, violet, primrose, and the snowdrop,
Springing up on every side—how lovely!
Just to say that Spring, indeed, is come!
Studded with these bright gems of heavenly purity,

Emulating buds in silent, happy struggle ;
The golden blossom, unparalleled in beauty
And unequalled in rich fragrance—blessed gifts !
Charming, smiling February, adieu ! adieu !
Thy days were short, but then thy fate was sealed.
Farewell ! calm happy month, even Nature speaks it !
Glowing March is come and bids thee go !
Each flowing month must follow to excel
In the precious gifts of glory's greatness.
Ah ! Nature's full of provident goodness !

But, stately March, what can be said of thee ?
O ! wouldst thou be superior in thy name ?
Thy character lies in thy marvellous goodness :
Thy howling winds in stormy play mysteriously
Scatter the flow'ry seed o'er the universe ;
And then thy March-dust, covering every atom,
Giving warmth and sweet unbroken stillness,
That April's gentle cheering showers may nourish.
Instilling life, to bloom and seed again !
O this exquisite grace—this quick'ning grandeur !
This godly duty, and triumphant greatness,
Can alone exalt a blessed name.
Most highly favoured month, indeed, thou art ;
So full of tender buds and growing beauty—
So full of light and truth-instructive knowledge,
That everything upon this blessed earth
Is passionately greeting thee,
And in one general anthem loud acclaim
The fulness of thy power—the greatness of thy name !

But stop! o'ercome in thought! thy life how short?
Ah! such is life—to make man think of Death:
In one still partial degree he welcomes thee,
In another, bids farewell to all thy greatness,
For Nature smiles the signal onward, March!
As other months, e'en thou must quickly go
And leave thy gain—thy honey-wine to flow.

    March 1st, 1861.

HAPPY MONTH OF MAY.

SWEET May, indeed, is come, full of beauty, power, and glory;
Thickly spreading invaluable treasure o'er the universe.
The world is richly clothed with bloom-fruitful blossom;
Heaven-exalted, blessed month, how full of joy!
The fairest forms and the brightest gems are given.
Which seem to delight in their shadow and song.
All things smile in love as they come and go;
They bid man watch the mighty hand of God,
Whose glorious law is holy, true and perfect.
By His divine control the earth rolls on;
In secret silence all things readily obey His word:
In the blissful passing moments through the year,
Each happy month in measured time appear,
And triumphantly unfold to man new gifts to cheer him.
How wonderful, astounding, indeed, the change—happy change!
Out of decay and waste spring life, light, and beauty.
Here is matchless proof of power and love divine,
To strengthen hope in man—immortal man.

Who is blessed indeed whilst here in mortal state.
For he beholds the great God in all things,
Which teach him to think more seriously of his soul,
Which is far more precious than the world's fair glory :
Everything is blessed with tender care and discipline.
How full of charms and smiles are the smallest flowers
As they wave their gentle heads, heavenward bowing,
And how lovely in infancy—how beautifully varied !
E'en the blades of grass, ivies, ferns, and downy moss,
The little weeds that are called into existence
To feed and to shelter countless minute beings.
Man may well look on in watchful prayer to God :
Here's living bread for the soul and mind to feed on :
Here man may hope in God and dream of Heaven,
Till faith and truth carry him thither.

May 6th, 1861.

SLANDER.

THE poisonous weed and thistle smile to waste,
And choke the blossom of the budding flower :
'Tis so with man who lives to please this world :—
He finds this bitter mixture in his cup,
The alloy of sin—heart-corroding sorrow,
To destroy his mental goodness, and the form
Of beauty God intended he should be
In youth and age. So in decline, alas !
His drooping head and languid heart is full
Of disappointment which the world gives
To influence, surely to destroy the soul,
By its alluring pleasures venom sweet.

Insensible to his greatness and his worth,
He deals in malice—oft in slander too,
Just to bring down pity from above ;
And vengeance from an offended God.

MISREPRESENTATIONS ; OR, PERSONAL WRONGS.

How often is the peace of mind disturbed
By a cruel serpent-headed fool—a spy !
Having no name himself, he covets others.
The wicked anonymous writer of the day,
Tho' the common wrongs of life no law can touch
Yet how beautiful is bold truth at all times !
The thorns of barren land deep in the mind ;
Nothing but truth alone can root them out.
What makes knavish prejudices hard to remove
Is, because we're praised and slandered by the knave,
(Such killing is no murder, 'tis only torture),
So charitable—kind always in the act

                            Of libelling some one.
But, alas ! how wrong is he who makes out wrong is right !
We mean the knave who only lives to slander,
Making white look black to suit his cause.
Every one should enjoy free liberty of speech ;
But only justified on the ground of truth.
Ah ! how studiously cautious men should be
To speak the sober truth of charity and love—
Not to cruelly misrepresent for the sake of gain.

June 29th, 1861.

NIGHT THOUGHTS.

THE evening shade must darken into night,
That Nature may become refresh'd, new-born,
To bear the holy Sun's sweet glowing light—
Ah ! quick'ning grace, to glorify the morn.

'Tis night—how still ! there's not a sound,
Adorning beauty smiles around ;
Behold the stars, shining to reveal
Their living light, no glory to conceal.

And then the beauty of our vision drawn,
The greater light, that holy light within,
Which lives to God eternally in peace
Of holy joys and love which never cease.

O, cheering thought !—we pass away,
In life's decline of unperceived decay,
To sleep in darkness till the coming day.

HIS WORD IS LOVE.

Do not all things speak the glorious praise
Of Him who bids the angel-light to go
And smile upon the germ to give it power
To unfold its truthful, unrevealed beauty ?
For by the touch of light all things are free.
To man God's willing hand gives ev'ry glory·--
So much of Heaven that he's forgetting Death,
And lives as if there were no other worlds ;
Often forgets his dear loving Maker :

But light approaches darkness day by day
To overturn the power of sin and Satan,
That man may be composed in his last hour—
How sweet the dissolution ! O how sweet !
Lulled to smiling sleep by angel-time,
Like the seed that's cast into the ground,
Which dies to give new life, power and beauty,
Awaken'd by the touch of angel-light
To live for ever in Paradisaical glory.

August 3rd, 1861.

THE HEAVENLY CALL.

THE angels of Innocence, Hope, and Love
By His word come forth with glory and power,
Just to smilingly welcome the Christian
To his last home of sacred rest and peace :
E'en Angel-Faith whispers his name in Heaven.
And bids him leave this world for joys more sweet.
The happy changeless beauty hereafter
Can ne'er die !   O, how wonderful, indeed,
Is that grand interchange of Holy Spirit—
Heavenly birth the crowning truth of light !
                    And does not man know
That His glorious law can ne'er deceive ?
Truthful, yea, blessed, is the Word of Him
Who bids *all* come to His Throne above,
And live with Him for ever in glory.

September 3rd. 1861.

LOVE AND HATRED.

"Just watch life's thistles bud and blow,—
    Oh ! 'tis a pleasant folly !
Alas ! when all our paths they sow,
    Then comes dread melancholy."
But love your foes if e'er you can,
For life, if long, is but a span,
To show the rotten fruits of man.
I love the honest and sincere,
    But hate the stuck-up proud,
Or those who live to domineer—
    Such glorians of the crowd.
But why, then, hate impulsive men,
    Who scoff behind one's back ?
To empty prayers repeat "Amen,"
    Self-righteousness they lack.
Such fiends who have the hidden knife
    Would cut down many an oak ;
The keenly blade of cutting strife
Might wound the smallest twigs of life,
    But who's to dread the stroke ?
Who lives for truth may care not for
    The giant-gnats so high,
Tho' insects will of course make war
    To tickle and to die.
As many idlers want a job,
    So learned quacks of light
May banter just to kill or rob,
    Or puzzle to delight.

I love a firm, sincere, old friend,
     But hate the double-face,
Whose busy tongue's deceit extends
     To triumph in disgrace.

WELCOME, FEBRUARY.

January, thou art gone, thy cruel reign is o'er;
Thy bitter smiles and unwelcome frowns have died away.
How many dear sons hast thou not taken with thee?
And where are they?—enduring calamity or tranquillity?
This question of time, alas! must be unanswered,
But the past must be forgotten. The wretched past
Is gone for ever, and why should we despair?
The rising of this beautiful month, serene,
Has brought a glimpse of never-failing Spring.
How welcome, beautiful February!—oh, how welcome!
Thy coming animates to life the drooping in despair.
How cheerfully, silently, expand the bursting buds,
Hushed into sweet delight—unutterable splendour!
Happy month, thou art too good to live long;
Thou giveth what another month would take—
O smiling, welcome February, thy gifts are great!

THE WORKING-BEE AND THE DRONE.

UNWELCOME drone !
Uninvited com'st thou forth to rob
  One of his labour, simply to distress
Th' industrious ! Ay, but does it not seem odd
Thou thou shouldst live to cheat, in sight of God,
  A little working-bee that would thee bless—
But were it not for such dishonest acts,
In taking tithes besides a heavy tax?

With eager joy the bee works hard for food :
  Not like the spider, which lives but for strife—
Inhuman monsters that have taste for blood,
  And cannot live unless they take the life
Of unoffending, helpless little flies,
Which only live to tickle and surprise.

          Alas, poor drone !
      Ah, thou despis'd one ! Charity must own.
Unwelcome guest ! ay, fruitless without power—
  Devouring all that comes within thy reach—
Canst thou not sip the honey-sweets from flower,
  And gain the knowledge smaller insects teach?

  Yet such is life : adventurous men exceed
  The limits of their reason ; tho', indeed,
  The world may treat with cold neglect and slight,
  Yet question whether black should not be white ;
  Though prejudice may sound her trumpet loud,
  No satire, wit, can move the ignorant proud :
  Does not the selfish miser starve to save
  Himself a little longer from the grave ?
    April 18th, 1865.

THE LILY AND THE DAISY.

In the language of a flower
Spake that little Lily-queen
Of sovereign magic power :—
" Little Daisy, condescend
To be the author of my end—
Hail, fellow-Daisy, hail !"
Behold the beauty of the vale :
A faded dying flower,
Whilst thou'rt full of living light.
Smiling in His power delight—
O ! heav'nly bloom—the Giver's art
Quick'ning beauty, grace impart,
Pure and spotless, bright become,
Holy for the Holy One.
Another day and thou'rt gone :
Then in death thy virtues learn—
All thy beauty shall return ;
For His light shall smile on thee
From time to all eternity.

May 11*th*, 1863.

AWAKE.

Awake ! why sleep to dream
Away the time that's given ?
Be watchful ; let thy theme
Be on the light of Heaven.

" Watch and pray," said He,
The God of holy care ;
Behold the Saviour—see
Him in the light of pray'r.
Rejoice, I say, rejoice,
In holy "watching" keep ;
O, listen to His voice ;
Awake, awake—why sleep?
In earnestness, yea, prove
A loving heart of light,
A praying soul of love,
In glory of delight.
O let thy spirit praise
His works of glory giv'n,
In holy faith to raise
Th' immortal soul to Heav'n !
Life's beauty soon is gone—
The fading flower of earth
May glorify the morn
And yet die in its birth.
Will man, alas ! will man,
Who only lives to die,
Secure new life ?—he can
By seeking God on high.
Oh ! sacred Light of Light,
Prepare the soul before
She takes her spirit-flight,
Here to return no more.
Then let us seek His light,
Whom all men should adore !

GOOD FRIDAY.

BEHOLD Him !
Nailed to the cross is He,
　　Amid the scoffs and jeers ;
See His violent agony,
　　Borne down in sorrow-tears ;
His persecutors standing by—
　　Gentile and wand'ring Jew.
Oh, listen to His mercy-cry,
　　" They know not what they do ;
Forgive them, Father ; oh, forgive
　　Them ; let Thy will be done !
Yea, let me die that all shall live !
　　Good God, Thy kingdom come !"
See Him bow His weeping head,
　　In prayer for every one.
" It is finished !" now he said ;
　　Oh, God, look on Thy Son !
To-day look on the Cross in love.
　　Alas ! His blood is shed
That we might live with Him above—--
　　He died, but is not dead !

Holy Week.

————◆————

WINTER.

THE with'ring foliage shows
Winter's come at last. The sky,
How dark and dreary ! what a change !
The snow and hail together lie,

To melt upon the earth—how strange—
Strangely beautiful appear,
All in harmony to raise,
Nature's living voice to cheer
The glowing season of the year
In triumph of His praise.

But Winter's come, to pass away,
And soon the smiling, cunning Spring
Will come to cheer, but not to stay ;
The secret signal of the day
Shows all in Nature must decay,
As seasons come and pass away.
'Tis so with man ; in time he's driven
By Death to living light of Heaven ;
For life-eternal joy is given
By Him who reigns supreme.

CONCLUSION.

My feeble,
Yet earnest, heavenward prayer shall be
That I've offended none :
I write for truth, but honestly,
To please friends every one,
Fearing neither friend nor foe :
An enemy I will not know,
Tho' I may want his love
Whilst groping in the dark below
For th' higher things above.
September 16*th*. 1870.

A FATHER'S LAMENT.

FAIR boy ! how cam'st thy lov'd form here entomb'd ?—
Four years scarce gone, thy birth two hearts illum'd
With radiant joys and hopes—ah, bright hopes rear'd
On thy sweet soul and love, which thee endear'd ;
Thy mental promise—ay, thy talents rare ;
Thy dauntless spirit, and thy prospects fair.

    Upheaving hearts suggest it cannot be
That thy entrancing smile, and youthful glee ;
Thy cherished, beauteous form ; thy golden hair ;
Thy just appreciation of parental care ;
Thy tender, loving grasp ; thy welcome greet ;
Thy captivating tongue ; thy sprightly gait ;
Thy intellectual fire ; thy beaming eye—
No more can cheer us here, nor wring a sigh
Lest harm shouldst thee befall,—lest thou shouldst die :-
A bud that blossom'd ere its time insur'd,
A mind develop'd ere the frame matur'd.

    But, oh ! this marble tells too true a tale :
Thy spirit's fled ; thou'st pass'd through Death's dark vale !-
Born but to charm, to love, be lov'd, and die—
Too good for earth,—fit for eternity.

    Yet still, bright thoughts o'er grief and sadness gleam :
Suppose this sorrow prov'd a flitting dream ;
Thy sweet voice heard again ; thy loving face
Beheld ; thy form clasp'd in life-long embrace :—
What joy !—ah, joy, not here, though yet to come
When, BERTIE, thou awak'st to greet us home.

A. M.

Kensal Green. October. 1869.

SUBSCRIBERS' NAMES TO THIS VOLUME.

The Right Worshipful the MAYOR of CANTERBURY, HENRY HART, Esq.

The Right Hon. LORD ATHLUMNEY (4 copies).

The Right Hon. LADY ATHLUMNEY.

H. A. BUTLER-JOHNSTONE, Esq., M.P.

The Right Rev. the BISHOP of DOVER.

The Very Rev. the DEAN of CANTERBURY.

The Ven. the ARCHDEACON of MAIDSTONE.

The Rev. the WARDEN of ST. AUGUSTINE'S.

Colonel HORSLEY, R.E.

The Rev. J. STEVENSON, D.D.

The Rev. C. MATHESON, Head Master, Clergy Orphan School.

The Rev. the PRECENTOR.

The Rev. T. HIRST, M.A.

A. MASEY, Esq., the "Globe."

Mrs. MASEY, 110, Strand.

The Rev. HENRY STEVENS, M.A.

The Rev. J. S. SIDEBOTHAM, M.A.

The Rev. EDGAR H. CROSS, M.A.

T. S. LIPSCOMB, Esq.

The Rev. R. G. HODGSON.

The Rev. J. B. WHITE, St. Stephen's.

W. H. LINOM, Esq.

Miss STEVENS, Deanery, Rochester.

Mrs. STEVENS, Wateringbury.

THOMAS WILKINSON, Esq., Best Lane.

W. H. D. BRADSHAW, M.B., &c.

GEORGE FURLEY, Esq.

GEORGE R. FREND, Esq., St. George's.

WALTER FURLEY, Esq., St. Margaret's.

Mrs. FOWLER, the Tower House.

JOHN ARIS, Esq., Canterbury.

Miss WARD, "Kentish Gazette."

Mr. HENRY SPRAGUE, Watling St.

Miss WEBB.

Mr. J. G. HALL, Architect and Surveyor, St. Margaret's.

Mrs. FAGG.

Miss A. SMITH.

F. ROOTS, Esq., Wincheap.

Mr. HENRY MILES, Canterbury.

Mr. TENCH WHITE, Music and Pianoforte Repository, St. George's Street.

THOMAS COOPER, Esq., Wincheap Street.

The Rev. W. TEMPLE, M.A.

The Rev. J. S. WATSON, M.A.

The Rev. E. GILDER, M.A.

Mr. C. J. AYRE.

THOMAS WHITE COLLARD, Esq.

JOHN DANCE, Esq.

J. R. COOPER, Esq.

Mr. GIBBS.

E. BRADLEY, Esq.

Dr. TUCKEY.

JOHN GEORGE DRURY, Esq.

GEORGE BEER, Esq.

WILLIAM WEIR, Esq.

Mr. ROBERT MILLS.

A. NEAME, Esq.

Mrs. GREENWOOD

l

Mr. J. COPPIN, Rose Hotel.
FRANCIS BATEMAN, M.B., &c.
Mr. THOS. CROUCH.
HERBERT T. SANKEY, Esq.
JAMES REID, Esq.
Mr. WALLACE GENTRY.
Mrs. HALL, St. Margaret's.
Mr. J. BATEMAN, St. George's Street.
Mr. HYDE.
Mr. A GOODBAN.
Mr. F. J. HOWARD.
Mr. E. JOY, Burgate Street.
F. R. BATEMAN, Esq.
Mr. J. POTTER, Builder, Rose Lane.
Mr. G. P. ARGRAVE, Burgate Street.
Mr. R. F. STRAND, King's Bridge.
WILKINSON BROTHERS.
W. W. FLINT, Esq., Leigh House, St. Dunstan's.
Mr. C. J. WOOD, St. Margaret's.
THOS. ASH, Esq.
EVAN LAKE, Esq., Solicitor.
Rev. C. A. FOWLER, M.A., St. Margaret's.
Mr. E. COLTHUP.
Mr. JOHN BISSENDEN.
Mr. W. T. HILL.
GEORGE SLATER, Esq.
Mr. H. B. WILSON.
Major-General MORTON, R.E.
THOS. HILTON, Esq., Nackington.
GEORGE MOUNT, Esq., Nackington.
ROBERT COLLARD, Esq., Nackington.
Mr. J. WILLEY.
W. K. CURTIS, Esq.
Mr. S. S. WARREN.
Mr. WM. ALDRIDGE.
Mr. THOS. JUDGE.
Mr. WILLIAM PARSONS.
Mr. W. MILES, Dane John.

The Rev. C. J. COAR, Chaplain to the Forces.
Mr. E. RIGDEN.
W. H. CULLEN, Esq., Lamb Lane.
T. G. BEER, Esq., Gravel Walk.
Mr. EDWARD HULSE, St. Peter's.
CHARLES HILLS, Esq., Solicitor.
Rev. J. MONK, St. Peter's Street.
Mr. J. H. HAMMOND, St. George's.
Mr. EDWARD WILLIAMS, Burgate Street.
Mr. HENRY BAKER.
Mr. ALFRED PHILPOTT, Burgate Street.
Mr. W. H. VILE, Burgate Street.
Mr. ROBERT COLLINS, Burgate St.
Mr. T. F. AVANN.
R. J. BELL, Esq., L.D.S.
R. PETTMAN, Esq., St. Margaret's.
Mr. HENRY CARTER.
Mr. ROBERT K. MOORHOUSE.
Mr. GEORGE HORAN, Castle Street.
Mr. G. E. TWYMAN.
Mr. W. PRETT, Palace Street.
Mrs. J. COWELL.
Mrs. NOBLE.
Miss F. GALE, Chantry House.
Mr. J. F. FILL, St. Peter's.
Mr. T. FETHERSTONE.
T. ASHENDEN, Esq., St. George's Terrace.
Z. PRENTICE, Esq.
Mr. E. PARKER, Northgate.
Mr. W. SWAIN, Northgate.
Mr. J. VAUTIER, Northgate.
Mrs. S. J. NOTLEY, Northgate.
Mr. WILLIAM BANISTER.
Mr. R. BETTS, Castle Street.
Mr. W. J. WHITE, Castle Street.
Mr. F. EDE, Castle Street.
Mr. J. REID, Castle Street.
Mr. GEORGE KIRBY, Castle Street.
Mr. F. BEASLEY, Stour Street.
H. WALLACE, Esq., St. Dunstan's.

J. MARTEN, Esq., Chilham.

Mr. ROBERT FULLFORTH.

Mrs. BURREN, Northgate.

ROBERT HAMILTON, Esq., St. Dunstan's Terrace.

Mr. WILLIAM WILKINSON, Bridge Street.

Mr. WALTER SHEEPWASH.

Mr. EDWIN BRENCHLEY.

Mr. WHIDDETT.

Mr. WM. RYE.

Mr. HENRY OVENDEN, St. Dunstan's.

Mr. B. ROFE, 3, Victoria Terrace.

Mr. T. SPURGEON COWTAN, St. Dunstan's.

Mr. AVANN.

Mr. WEBB, St. Dunstan's.

Mrs. RAMMELL, Monastery House, Longport.

Miss NEAME, St. Dunstan's.

Mr. WILLIAM HAMES, St. Dunstan's.

Mrs. W. WACHER, Herne.

PHILIP JACKSON, Esq., 15, Grand Parade, St. Leonard's-on-Sea.

Mr. J. S. HIGGINS, Clifton House, Canterbury.

Mr. R. STROUTS, St. Dunstan's.

Mrs. JERMAINE, St. Dunstan's.

Miss NEWPORT, Bridge Street.

Mr. ALFRED JONES.

Rev. W. BIRD, St. Dunstan's.

Mr. CHARLES PETERS, Canterbury.

Mr. T. U. SOUTHEE, St. Dunstan's Terrace.

Mr. E. WILLCOCKS, Broad Street.

Mr. W. COGGER, Broad Street.

Mrs. JOHNSON, Barton Mills.

Mrs. E. ELLIS, Oaten Hill.

JOHN BRENT, Esq., F.S.A.

Mr. WILLIAM GILLMAN.

Mr. JOSEPH WILSON, Cossington.

Mr. J. H. WOODGATE.

Mr. J. S. STIFF, Broad Street.

Mr. R. PILCHER, Oaten Hill.

Rev. N. HOWARD MCGACHEN.

LADY GREY DE RUTHYN.

Miss THOMAS, 16, St. George's Terrace.

Mrs. FOREMAN, 9, St. George's Terrace.

Mr. ISAAC RATCLIFF, 3, Riding Gate Watling Street.

GEORGE ASH, Esq., Jun., Old Dover Road.

Mr. GEORGE EDWARD DITCH, St. Margaret's Street.

Mr. THOMAS BATES, Broad Street, Canterbury.

Mr. CHARLES AYERS, Dover Street, Canterbury.

Mr. EDWARD ROBERTS, Broad Street, Canterbury.

Mr. T. DOBSON, King Street.

Mrs. WALKER, St. George's Street.

GEORGE ASH, Esq., Watling St.

Mr. W. H. VERRALLS.

Mrs. HYDER, St. George's Place.

Mr. HENRY SOUTHEE, 3, St. Dunstan's Terrace.

Mrs. FREND.

Miss COOPER, Bridge Street.

Mr. W. R. PRETT, Northgate.

Mr. JOHN BRYSON, Palace Street.

R. Y. FILL, Esq., St. George's Place.

Captain STEAD, St. Stephen's Road.

Miss HAWLEY.

Mr. CHARLES HARNDEN, Broad Street.

Mr. KEEN, Rhodaus Town.

Mr. PETTIT, St. George's.

Mr. EDWARD SWAIN, St. Dunstan's.

Mr. WILLIAM GEORGE, Bridge Street.

Mr. JACKSON, High Street.

Rev. G. W. TEMPLE.

Mr. E. WILKINSON, High Street.

W. D. FURLEY, Esq.
Rev. Mr. WILLIAMS.
Mr. GEORGE COTTRELL, Bridge St.
Mr. C. SMITH SMITH, Burgate St.
Mr. W. WRAIGHT, Orange Street.
Mr. MARSHALL, Burgate Street.
MATTHEW BELL, Esq., Bourne Park.
Mr. EDMUND GIBBS, Bridge.
Mr. HENRY CORNES, Bridge.
Mr. HENRY VYE, Glens Falls, Bridge.
Mrs. W. FAGG, Bridge.
Mr. HENRY AUSTEN, Bridge Terrace.
Miss PARKER, Hill-Side, Bridge.
Mrs. BETTS, Bridge.
REST WILLIAM FLINT, Esq., 5, St. George's Place.
H. MORRIS, Esq., Bridge.
Miss L. R. BUNDOCK, St. Margaret's.
Miss WATSON.
Mrs. FORD, Palace Street.
Mr. THOMAS ANDREWS, Friars.
Messrs. WILLIAMSON and SON.
Mr. THOMAS CRUMP, Mercery Lane.
Mr. R. G. DIXON, Croydon.
Mr. A. WALLACE, Court Hill Road, Lewisham.
Mr. ROBERT GODDEN, Castle St.
Mr. JAMES FOLWELL, Castle Street.
Mr. ELLEN, Castle Street.
Hr. HENRY PENSON.
Mrs. CHISHOLM.
Mr. HENSON.
Mr. R. PORT, Hanover Place.
Mr. B. ANDREWS, 8, Hanover Place.
Captain DUNCAN, Hanover Place.
JOHN HAWLEY, Esq., Brunswick House Academy, Leamington.

Mr. JAMES FEDARB, St. Peter's Street.
Mr. THOMAS FOSTER, Academy, Hanover Place.
Miss PARKER, Hanover Place.
Mr. B. M. CHITTENDEN, St. Dunstan's.
Mr. THOMAS WARR, 2, St. Dunstan's Street.
Mr. ORCHARD, St. Margaret's St.
Mr. G. BOURNE, Broad Street.
G. R. JOHNSON, Esq., Sturrey.
W. R. RAMMELLS, Esq., Sturrey.
Miss MURRELL, Sturrey.
Colonel COX, Fordwich.
Mr. FRED. KERREY, Colchester.
H. AUSTEN, Esq., Archbishop's Palace, Canterbury.
Mr. CASSELL, Palace Street, Canterbury.
Mr. THOMAS PETTS, St. Dunstan's, Canterbury.
Miss FRANCIS, Upper Bridge St., Canterbury.
WILLIAM WATSON MASON, Esq., Barton Fields.
Mr. JAMES HOWARD, Bridge Street.
W. BLAXLAND, Old Park Farm.
C. COLLARD, Esq., Little Barton.
Mr. A. SARGENT, Berkesbourne.
J. C. HUKINS, Esq.
Mr. A. GINDER, St. George's Hall, Canterbury.
Mr. JORDAN, St. Peter's Street.
Mr. W. E. GOULDEN, High Street, Canterbury.
Mr. GEORGE HOLLOWAY, Chartham.
Mr. JOHN HARVEY, Burnt House, Chartham.
HENRY COLLARD, Esq., Wincheap.
Mr. HENRY PAINE, St. Peter's Place.
Mr. PHILLIPS, Canterbury.

www.ingramcontent.com/pod-product-compliance
Lightning Source LLC
Chambersburg PA
CBHW020810060726
47498CB00017B/1428